PHASE SIX

PHASE SIX

Jim Shepard

riverrun

First published in the United States in 2021 by Alfred A Knopf
First published in Great Britain in 2021 by

riverrun

An imprint of

Quercus Editions Limited
Carmelite House
50 Victoria Embankment
London EC4Y 0DZ

An Hachette UK company

A CIP catalogue record for this book is available
from the British Library.

Hardback ISBN 978 1 52941 507 0
Trade Paperback ISBN 978 1 52941 508 7
Ebook ISBN 978 1 52941 510 0

10 9 8 7 6 5 4 3 2 1

Printed and bound in Great Britain by Clays Ltd, Elcograf S.p.A.

Papers used by Quercus are from well-managed forests and other responsible sources.

For James Ewing and Milla Riggio,
who refused to give up on me—

We do not see our hand in what happens, and so we call certain events melancholy accidents . . .

—STANLEY CAVELL

Our responsibility is historic, for when the history of AIDS and the global response is written, our most precious contribution may well be that at the time of the plague we did not flee; we did not hide; and we did not separate.

—JONATHAN MANN

Everyone has a plan until they get punched in the mouth.

—MIKE TYSON

Gentlemen, it is the microbes who will have the last word.

—LOUIS PASTEUR

I

✦ ✦ ✦ ✦ ✦ ✦ ✦ ╬ ✦ ✦ ✦ ✦ ✦ ✦ ✦ ✦ ✦ ✦ ✦

HIS FATHER'S EXPRESSION

It had gotten colder overnight, and the gravediggers had had to use a pneumatic drill. Aleq had had to listen to it all morning.

The Hansenips and the Jorgensens and their cousins and some of the Geislers smoked and talked during the procession to the grave-yard, and Aleq and Malik trailed along behind, Malik on his phone. They had no Wi-Fi in Ilimanaq but he downloaded stuff when he went to Ilulissat.

The Lange family all stood off to one side of the shallow hole with the coffin in it while their kids played around the graves. Malik asked without looking up if Aleq wanted to join the club called Everyone Hates Aleq, and Aleq watched two three-year-olds down the hill piss on the same spot in the snow and said he was already a member.

Some of the grave sites had little white fences around them and some were just white crosses among the rocks. Some of the graves had seashells on them and some had plastic flowers or wreaths. While the minister talked, Aleq and Malik scrolled through pictures of other people's pets and vacations. Aleq's grandmother gave him a look, so he stepped away and lifted his head like he was interested in some-thing else. By the time the minister finished it was sleeting, so when the service was over, a lot of people headed back to their houses and the family almost had to fill in the grave alone. When Aleq looked back, the wind was blowing even the frozen dirt off their shovels. When he looked back again, halfway down the hill, they'd finished with the dirt and had rolled all of the large stones on top and were posing for their photographs with their hoods up. One of the girls in the family waved—he couldn't even tell which twin from that far away—but he kept his hands stuffed in his anorak.

An older kid named Tavik was ahead of them heading down the hill. "Want to see the most stupid expression in Greenland?" Malik asked him. When the kid looked up, Malik pointed at Aleq.

"Just West Greenland," the kid told him. "I have a cousin in Tasiilaq who's worse than that."

The kid went on ahead and left them behind. Malik had his phone to his ear, and even with the wind you could hear a little music. "Is that Baba Saad?" Aleq asked. They liked German gangsta rap and Malik liked to sing it, though nobody liked to listen. Sometimes he lost interest in the middle of a question, and if you asked the same question twice, he paced, like it had taken you too long to figure out what you needed to know.

The sleet stopped, and down by the water they found a patch free of bottles and feathers and sat on a rock, so close to the water's edge they had to lift their feet every so often for the choppy little waves. It didn't get fully dark, but on cloudy days the brightest glow in the sky was to the north, and to the west the moon was so low it was sitting on Disko Island. Out past the cement wharf old man Rosbach bobbed around in an open boat filled with a new tied-down ATV. Eventually the crane operators winched it up. They had also just hauled up a mini-fridge that one of the Villadsens was dragging over to his own ATV on a sheet of cardboard to keep it from being scratched on the cement.

Two of the chained dogs closest to Aleq and Malik ignored them, and two howled. Aleq threw some pebbles at the howlers, and then at Malik, and then they tried hitting each other's legs by skipping flat rocks off the rock they were sitting on. It was the kind of stupid game that left them nicked up and bloody under their pant legs and made Aleq's grandmother mad, like when they played You're It on the steep slopes above open water. Or the way they were always running around after dark and looking in people's windows. Though whatever they were doing was usually Aleq's idea, they got in equal trouble, and he felt bad about that, but it was like his heart was always the happiest when they were up to something they weren't supposed to be doing.

BE GOOD OR THE QIVITOQ WILL GET YOU

When they got back to his grandmother's house they stood outside in the wind while Malik finished looking at something on his phone, and finally Aleq went inside. His grandmother was cleaning, and when he asked why, she told him that after the Hansenips and Geislers called on the family, they were going to come by for coffee and cake. "Where's your friend with the answers?" she asked. She'd started calling Malik that after he'd started saying "I don't know" whenever she asked him a question. While she was talking Malik came through the door fussing with finding a pocket for his phone. "Now look what they've done," he said when he saw the table set up with all the food and wine and coffee, like it was his house.

Aleq hung their coats on nails and to help out lined up their black rubber boots beside the plastic buckets along the entry room wall. So many people came in behind them that they were pushed all the way over to the open wooden chest his grandparents used to keep everything in. They sat on its edge, and Malik in his boredom pulled out a piece of hide, a harpoon head, a pad of paper, and a set of earphones. The front door kept banging open and then someone would shut it again. More people squeezed in and moved around the house. Almost everyone was smoking, and there was one bad smell after another depending on who was standing nearby. Aleq's grandmother saw him moving away from people and gave him another look. She told everyone he had a sensitive nose. Where'd he *get* a nose like that? she wanted to know. No one else in the settlement had one.

His grandfather's rule was that in his own house he got to be comfortable, so he was in his long underwear and slippers. The elastic had worn out in the sleeves and ankles. Malik called him Mr. Wolf after the Danish fashion magazine. Malik never asked what it was like to have been adopted by your grandparents because your father and mother hadn't been married or had a house of their own. They finally had gotten married when Aleq was eight, and now they had three other kids. He visited sometimes and had slept there once when his grandmother had had her sister's family over. Malik's family was related to everybody, but it seemed like Aleq's family wasn't related to anybody. It didn't matter, though, because in a year he'd have to leave for middle school in Ilulissat anyway.

Malik came back from the table with a cup of the wine Aleq's grandmother called Three Seals because of the shape on the label, and she was right behind him and took it out of his hand. "Be good or the qivitoq will get you," she said over the noise. Malik said a qivitoq was way too busy to worry about someone like them, but it scared them anyway and his grandmother knew it. His grandfather had seen one that had killed three dogs and was always stealing char from the drying racks at his fishing camp. He said the best way to spot them was on the ridgelines against the sky. They'd been men or women who'd had problems with other people or been unlucky in love and had gone off to live in the mountains and after they'd died had stayed as ghosts. His grandfather said the one he saw had white and mottled skin that was horribly loose and long hair and even longer nails. In the winter they scared you by looking in your windows. There were whole areas in the mountains where no one went because of them. The new mine was in the mountains, and Malik had brought that up when Aleq had told him about where they could sneak under the fence, but when Aleq had shamed him about being afraid, Malik hadn't mentioned it again.

SPRING, EXCEPT NOT REALLY

For two days it was even colder and then for a week it was so warm everyone went out in shirtsleeves. The ice in the corners of the entryway in his grandmother's house melted from the sunshine through the windows. They rode their bikes through slush rivers in the streets so deep their pedals were underwater. All the rocks were slippery with meltwater and the air had that smell of the beginning of summer and everything thawing out.

Malik wanted to see what was so cool about the mine before they went back there at night. There was supposed to be a bigger mine on Disko Island but one had also been started past the lake and up in the hills way to the east. The road past the cemetery went all the way south to Qasigiannguit and the track for the mining company went off it up and over the ridge. There was a No Trespassing sign on a sawhorse where the track left the road. The sand turned to mud as you went past the cemetery and down the hill, but you could bike around it.

It was far enough even on the bikes that they had to take a break, and looked back toward the town. Up higher even in the sun there was just enough cold in the air. Back below the cemetery, some women carried full plastic bags up the hill and an ATV roared past them and some teenagers drinking on the picnic tables.

"This better be good," Malik said, making a face at all the climbing they still had to do.

THE GREEN ECONOMY

Some fifteen years earlier the government of Greenland had announced that it had approved four times the number of mining exploration licenses granted in the previous decade. An Australian company had already begun zinc and lead mines on the northern coast, and fifty-six other active licenses were granted for gold, rubies, nickel, copper, and rare earth minerals, including neodymium, praseodymium, dysprosium, and terbium. The mines were promoted as contributing to the green economy, since 80 percent of the rare earth deposits would be used in wind turbines, hybrid cars, and lasers, so the pitch became "Global Warming and Greenland: We're Part of the Solution." Instead of publicizing a lot of moping and moaning Inuits trooping off to international conferences to lament the destruction of their fishing grounds, why not focus on the resources that native geologists were discovering every day under the vanishing ice sheets? Either you sat and just reacted to what was hurtling toward you, or you worked to get ahold of whatever opportunity brought along. Every settlement council had its visionaries who could anticipate hundreds of generated jobs and new airports and roads and hotels. When it was pointed out that 90 percent of the world's rare earth minerals came from China and that the environmental degradation those mines had left behind was stunning, the glass-half-empty types were refuted with the reminder that the goal of self-sufficiency had to trump the notion of a continent changed beyond recognition, and were further chided that they couldn't live in a museum, and that the country was so huge, how could a few mines make a difference?

With that door now wide open, Bluejay Mining, based in London and Frankfurt, had announced that it was initiating a nickel-copper-platinum-cobalt-sulfide project in the Disko Bay area, which had already been the subject of more than three decades of mining exploration, and that it was confident of proving up the region's resource potential.

The environmental and social impact assessments had been completed with the help of independent consultants from Denmark who, it turned out, had entered into discreet but fruitful partnerships with the mining companies. Greenlanders had been informed that they had been walking on billions of dollars all their lives and had never known it. What was a country to do when the traditional way of life no longer paid the bills? As Aleq's grandfather sometimes complained, many were unemployed. Families were moving away. It would be nice to see citizens doing something other than drinking wine and walking around in circles.

THIS THING OF DARKNESS

Malik had liked what he'd seen of the new mining camp, three cargo containers with doors that he and Aleq guessed were offices and two tents on the bare rock around a big hole dug in the permafrost, with one of those sectional chain link fences that anyone could slide under. He especially liked the drill rig, which had been floated in on a barge with its own crane while the whole settlement had watched, and which almost hadn't made it over the ridge despite being pulled by a giant thing with tracks like their snowmobiles, which had also had to come in on a barge.

The drill rig had been taller than the top of their church steeple, but they hadn't gotten very close before they'd been shooed away by a foreman in a green hard hat who'd headed toward them flapping his hand, so they'd waited a few nights before going back. Then Aleq left his grandparents snoring into each other's faces and met Malik in front of the cemetery and they rode all the way back out to the mine. Once they were well into the hills, he could see Malik keeping an eye out for the qivitoq, which his grandfather had also for their benefit called the "taaqtoq," or "This Thing of Darkness," to make it even scarier.

"Do you think the mining company has cameras?" Malik asked once they got there. They were still sweating from all the hills. They laid their bikes down and crouched, and Aleq asked himself what they were crouching for. He led Malik up to the fence, watching for anything that looked like a camera. The fence was held in place by cement blocks piled with big rocks, so it was easy to move and slide under.

They could smell rain, but it wasn't raining yet. The wind picked up and his nose ran. The plastic sheets that weren't tied down over the equipment whipped and snapped and the tent walls bowed in. There was a big toolbox near the tents, but it was locked with a padlock. Malik spent a lot of time by the drill rig, but Aleq went over to the pit. He got on his belly and put his chin on the edge and the cold air coming up from the blackness below rolled over him like water. Down that low, besides the dirt and broken stone, he could smell the crowberry stalks and bunting scat. He climbed the giant pile of excavated permafrost, and when Malik saw him making landslides by jumping downward he came running over. They slogged up to the very top and sat. Malik burrowed his butt in and stuck his legs out, recognizing the silence of someone else's happiness. Then he pushed Aleq a little ways down the pile and Aleq stayed where he stopped, his face in the dirt.

THIS THING OF DARKNESS

They visited the camp the next three nights, and on that fourth night, back on the dirt pile, Aleq showed Malik a rock he'd unearthed with some digging that was glassy smooth on one side from the polish Ice

Age glaciers had given it eleven thousand years earlier. But what had also caught Aleq's attention was a cavity where the surface had been spalled off, a scar of fractured crystals of feldspar and hornblende and ancient ice. Aleq had been taken with the contrasting textures and had brought his friend's palm over to experience the difference between polish and edge. Two days earlier, the drill bit's relentless pounding on the rock had finally broken the chemical bonds holding it to its ledge, and when that seam had cracked and the stress boundaries had separated, a cluster of molecules that had previously thrived in the respiratory tract of an early variant of the Bering goose and that had been trapped with some throat tissue in the crystalline framework during the Holocene glaciation had been reintroduced to the air and the warming sun. Even lying there in the darkness and dirt, Aleq could smell them, like heated metal. He had Malik smell, too, those molecules that were now released to become a part of something new.

BUTTONHOLES

The next day they both had sore throats and made fun of how much their noses were running. It rained so much you could hear the run-off on the road from inside the house. It was the weekend, so Aleq headed over to Malik's without waiting for breakfast. When he got there the rain had let up and Malik's mother was out front plucking ptarmigan, and the wind was so strong the feathers she released just disappeared. Malik's father was replacing some rotten duckboards leading up to the house. When you stood on them they teetered on the cottongrass that was humped from the snowmelt. The ones leading into the house were more of a mess than most.

They lived out by the rubbish dump for everything that wouldn't burn, and their chimney didn't draw very well no matter how many times Malik's father cleaned it, and the smoke always blew in your face. Inside Malik was watching a movie with his brothers and didn't look up. Even with his boots off Aleq didn't know where to step. The parents slept on a mattress on the floor with the baby, and the boys were in bunk beds in the bedroom three to a bunk, but everyone's stuff was everywhere. The clothes box was on its side and pants and mittens and sealskin gloves had been kicked all around. The baby was playing in a pile of old clothes. She had knitted booties and wet black bangs and tipped over and pawed the air.

Malik's older brother came out of the bedroom and left. He worked the shit truck emptying house buckets and liked the job because it was good money and finished early so he could go hunting. Something weird was happening in the movie so Aleq crossed the mattresses and sat down and Malik's little brothers looked him over. One was short and easy to scare and the other was mean with sharp little teeth. Malik was wearing the short one's favorite hat. A while ago he'd started what he called doing business with them, and always ended up with most of their things. Aleq said hello, and Malik said hello back after his dad came in singing. He sang songs about summer arriving or people doing themselves in. He finished one song and asked Malik what he was doing, and Malik said that to make his shirt fit better he was cutting new buttonholes with his knife. His father asked if he wanted help, and when Malik didn't answer he said in an old-fashioned way that he didn't appreciate Malik's attitude. Malik said that *he* didn't like the sounds his father and mother had made the night before, and his father explained that those were the sounds of an expert at work. Malik just kept watching the movie, and his father finally added that it was only when you were *really* depressed that you learned how to be a Greenlander.

"That kid from the cemetery ran into me on his bike," Aleq told Malik.

"You never use people's names," Malik complained. "You're the only person in the settlement that doesn't. You just say 'that guy,' or 'that kid.' It's weird."

"I'm weird," Aleq reminded him. Malik gave him a look.

When Malik's father finished what he was doing, he went back outside, and Malik's brothers got bored and followed, so then it was just the two of them, and the baby in the clothes. "You're the best friend I ever had," Aleq said, surprising himself, and Malik smiled at him with his runny nose, like he knew everyone was sad, or had been, or soon would be, and that that had made him grateful that Aleq was around. Later that night his look came back to Aleq when Aleq was helping haul the outboard motor out of storage. "What're *you* smiling at?" his grandfather asked.

INTERNATIONAL RELATIONS

Sunday morning they went down to the water near the old halibut factory and sat in their favorite spot on one of the cement wharves built into the rock. Near where the cable for the hand winch for dragging boats or whales up onto the ramp ran into the water, a dead dog floated under the ice. Aleq wiped his nose with his sleeve and then wiped Malik's. Around lunchtime they walked back to the supermarket in the middle of the settlement and sat on the big flat rocks where the brook became a waterfall into the harbor, and some of the mine workers showed up and sat next to them and started eating and drinking.

Other kids had followed the mine workers there, but kept their distance. Visitors usually had one or two kids behind them, since if you hung out near them they sometimes gave you their weird candy or food.

The wind off the water helped with the mosquitoes. Three of the mine workers were white and one was dark skinned. The foreman recognized Aleq and nodded at him and Aleq and Malik were close enough to hear their talk. Some were speaking Danish and some something else. Aleq's Danish was better than his grandparents', since they figured that only teachers and midwives and young people needed to make themselves understood in that language, and maybe mechanics, since they were always ordering parts. The foreman seemed interested in teasing them and kept running his hands through his own hair, so Malik pretended to be thrilled and told him, "You're *so* tall and *handsome*," and then was happy when the foreman and two of the men laughed. Then the dark-skinned worker showed them a funny video he'd taken of one of his drunk white friends falling down a flight of stairs, and the mine workers talked about getting to go home the next day. They were happy about it. Then the dark-skinned worker and Malik showed each other their phones. And the mine workers shared some Danish bread they had bought at the supermarket and some snow crab they had gotten at the tourist restaurant. Everyone loved the snow crab and there was a lot of it so it was passed around. And in that way their shared fork became a fomite, from the Latin *fomites*, for tinder, or fire starter: an object that when contaminated with an infectious agent will transfer that agent to the new host.

NOBODY FEELS VERY GOOD TODAY

In the morning, all of the dogs were howling but there was nothing out on the water and Aleq couldn't see anything up in the hills. No one was awake except some smaller kids who were jumping on a discarded oil tank by the lake and trying to get it to rock. He walked over to Malik's and everyone there was up though no one was outside. Malik's mother was making something on the stove and told

Aleq that Malik couldn't see anybody today and that he'd been shaking so much his brothers had let him have the bed. Malik shouted from the bedroom to let Aleq in, and his mother shrugged, and went back to the stove.

The bedroom had the shades down and had a different smell and one of Malik's little brothers looked sick, too. "You okay?" Aleq asked, and sat near Malik's head. The little brother was lying on the floor and Malik was so sweaty his hair was soaked. He was scrolling through his phone without really looking at it: some selfies, a skate park. He gave Aleq a look like they had nothing to worry about. There was white stuff around his mouth. His other little brother was out in the kitchen, and they heard his mother tell him that if he did that again she would bite him to death. On the wall under the bunk Malik had pasted up photos from magazines: basketball players and swimsuit models.

He was shaking like something cold was coming from inside him. "I'm glad I didn't make *you* sick," he said, looking at Aleq. His father heard him and stuck his head in the room. "You need the bucket?" he asked. He looked terrible himself. He saw Aleq notice, and said, "It's like what the starving seal says after the hunter misses him: 'Well, nobody feels very good today.'"

Malik's mother said from the kitchen that his father should try some of the medicine she was making, and he called, "How about I go my way and you go yours?" and that shut her up.

Aleq found a T-shirt and helped Malik wipe his face and stayed with him until it was clear that his friend felt bad enough that he was better off at least trying to sleep. Malik tried to get him to stay, and wanted to tell him something, but he ended up coughing so much that he finally couldn't. Aleq told him he'd come back after lunch. By the time Aleq was telling him that, Malik couldn't even hold his phone, and his little brother was off playing with it. When

Aleq waved from the doorway, Malik gave him a thumbs-up, but had his lower lip stuck out the way it did when something had him confused.

BIG BOY SICKNESS

When Aleq got back home, his grandfather was bent over outside on the road with a jar of mustard in one hand and a can of motor oil in the other. When he saw Aleq, he complained that the store was out of potatoes and margarine but you could always buy a CD player. In the kitchen he bent over again, and said that this was no weakling sickness that was going from house to house. This was a big boy sickness. His grandmother went straight to their bed and pulled out the trunk from underneath and handed him her mother's big red scarf that she said was guaranteed to get rid of sickness. Her family was hardier than his and they knew what was what, she reminded him. He said that his family was as hardy as anybody's and she reminded him that her people came from so far north that their word for winter was also the word for a year. She sat him down and tied the scarf around his neck, and then after a while he said he felt worse, so she went back to the supermarket herself to get some stuff for soup. While she was gone he climbed into bed. Aleq asked if his grandfather wanted him to hang around, and his grandfather said, "Who am I, your father? Have I ever told you how to spend your time?" His grandmother came back with beer, canned meat, and teabags, and by the time Aleq was leaving she was starting a stock with the canned meat.

MISS PAARMA IN OVER HER HEAD

It rained so hard three days later the puddles looked like they were boiling. Aleq stood under an overhang and watched the Hansenips' dogs burrow under each other for shelter. When the rain let up and he went back to Malik's, only Malik's mother was there, worrying about the baby. She said that Malik and his father and brothers were at Miss Paarma's.

Miss Paarma was the health service nurse who had a few beds and a medicine box in her back room and was supposed to phone the hospital to figure out what to do for sick people who weren't going to be moved to Ilulissat, or sometimes even to decide when to call for the helicopter. When Aleq got to her house she didn't answer the door, but the key was always on a hook in the shed so he let himself in. People were piled on the blue sofas in her waiting room and filled the rooms next door as well. The back room was packed beside the beds and he had to step over three kids and an old person lying in the entryway. Miss Paarma stuck her head out of the room in the way back to see what was going on. She usually had her hair in the traditional style though she also wore lipstick and Ray-Bans even in the house, but it looked like someone had gotten her up in the middle of the night. She was on the phone and wasn't happy about it. She told him he should leave and then seemed to forget when he didn't listen. Everyone there was shaking and soaked and coughing and having trouble breathing, except one woman who, when he looked at her, said that she'd been bitten in the face by her husband. She had a herder's smell—smoke, meat, and mildew—but everyone else smelled of something else. It was stronger than the seaweed and boiled meat broth on the stove.

Miss Paarma was talking to herself about a number she couldn't find and stuck her face next to her computer screen and then dumped out her purse on her desk, and he noticed how worn her wallet was at the corners while she fished through a roll of mints and some pens. In the back room Malik was shoulder to shoulder against the wall with his father and one of his little brothers. His other little brother was flat on the floor on his face.

"What do they have?" Aleq asked her. "Is this like that thing from China?" He'd been little when that thing had gone around the world, but he'd been told about it.

She said it seemed different. She knelt next to Malik's little brother on the floor and felt his neck with two fingers and told Aleq if he wanted to help he should get out of here because it was probably catching, and he could take her cell phone and keep trying to get through to the hospital in Ilulissat because her Wi-Fi was coming and going. She pointed to the phone on the desk. She said she'd keep trying on email and when he did get through he should tell them she had thirteen cases too serious to deal with here that had to go to Ilulissat if not Nuuk or Copenhagen. He asked if Malik was okay and she told him that *none* of them were okay, and then when he stayed near her she yelled at him to go.

He climbed to higher ground and stood out in the wind calling but he didn't get through. While he called he watched people come and go outside the nurse's house, most of them in a panic about their friends and relatives.

SO THAT WAS NO HELP AT ALL

By the time he got cold enough to get tired of calling and brought the phone back and made his way through the people waiting outside the nurse's house, one of Malik's little brothers had stopped breathing and so had his father and so had two of the kids on the floor of the entryway. The nurse had one of them on his back on her lap and was crying and breathing into his mouth and thumping his chest. Aleq worked his way through the rooms to Malik, who still seemed the same as before. The people outside were alarmed and upset and some were ducking inside in pairs and hoisting up their relatives and carrying them out and home.

BECAUSE MICROBES RUN THE WORLD

What health professionals label as pathogens are just microbes exploiting a new resource but otherwise doing what they've been doing for three billion years: feeding, growing, and spreading. Under optimal conditions they can double their numbers every half hour. They don't die until something kills them, and they thrive everywhere and have been brought up alive from the bottom of the Marianas Trench, from beneath ice a mile thick in Antarctica, and from strata 140 million years old in a drill core two miles deep. Left to their own devices, most reside unnoticed in biological balance with their ecosystems. But what location on earth remains left to its own devices? In an estuary, *Vibrio cholerae* is a blandly productive member of its community, but scooped up into the body in a drink of water, it can empty a human being of thirty liters of fluid a day.

THE WORST THING EVER

Aleq's grandparents blamed themselves for getting sick and argued about having chosen the wrong medicines to keep the sickness away. They were shaking and sweating and wrapped together in their biggest blanket, his grandmother holding it closed with her fist. Aleq asked if he could get them anything and his grandmother coughed so much she couldn't answer but his grandfather asked for one of his little beers. He liked them because he could finish them before they got warm. Before Aleq left he put a video on for them, and his grandmother remembered the way movies used to be shown in the community hall without subtitles and someone would just explain what was going on.

When he got back to Miss Paarma's, Malik's mother and older brother had taken Malik home. Miss Paarma was still on the computer, and it looked like a lot of the people on the floor in the back room had been dragged together and covered with sheets and blankets. Back at Malik's he let himself in and the older brother was gone and it was just Malik's mother going back and forth trying to help Malik.

Aleq sat with him, but Malik didn't seem to see him. Food appeared on his lap and then was taken away. Aleq reminded him of the way, on bad-weather days, they used to tell each other that if they closed their eyes and opened them again, the sun would be back out.

Finally Malik moved his arms and opened his eyes. His head swayed like they were on a boat.

"How're you feeling?" Aleq asked.

Malik smiled a little. He nodded, and then seemed to realize that that wasn't an answer. "Better," he whispered. "Better already."

He seemed to want to lie back, and Aleq helped him. There wasn't a good enough place for his head. Aleq asked if he wanted water and Malik blinked like he did when he was surprised by something. The bedroom floor was wet, and Aleq could feel it seeping into his pants. He found Malik's phone and they looked at animal pictures while his mother came and went, crying.

"Fix your face," Malik whispered to him. "It's all scrunched up." He was shaking so hard Aleq didn't know where he got the strength. He put his face against Malik's cheek. It was so hot that he could feel the heat before he even got close.

After a while Malik's mother came back in and moved Aleq aside, and grabbed Malik and put her head to his chest and started wailing. Aleq knelt next to them, shocked, and then said, "He's okay," though he knew it was like Malik's body had been trying and trying to get stronger and then had just stopped. He stood and circled the rooms and found himself in the bathroom. In the mirror he was open mouthed and teary.

He could hear Malik's mother outside. It sounded like she was headed away from the house. He went back to where Malik was lying and slid his friend's phone under an arm, and then sat on the lower bunk like he was waiting for something else. He could hear more crying coming from other parts of the settlement.

He'd taken off his boots at the door and his socks were as wet as his knees, so he pulled Malik's beat-up summer Nikes out of the clothes box at the foot of the bed and held them in front of him, and then pulled them on. And then he decided that his feet felt better anyway.

AVEDA GROOMING CLAY

Three days before that, on the morning all the sled dogs spent howling, the foreman for Bluejay Mining's Rare Earth Elements Disko Bay II Mine, Christian Leine, and five of his crew were the last ones aboard an Air Greenland flight that after two stops dropped them exhausted at Keflavík International Airport in Reykjavík. They were each becoming histological messes. They had completed the verification drilling on schedule and had weathered their double shifts with the union's blessing and had earned their paychecks and their two weeks home. It wasn't clear yet whether the higher-ups were going to settle on ion exchange or multi-stage solvent extraction or what, but there'd be multiple steps in the separation process, and that wasn't their worry, anyway, being a concern way above their pay grade, though it sounded like they would be doing some of that work onsite in order to save transportation costs on so many tons of permafrost.

Christian was so overheated that he was sweating on the plane, especially before they got moving, and the air nozzle above his seat didn't seem to be working at all, and when he wiped himself down with the little napkins the stewardesses handed out, he apologized to the old lady sitting next to him. She seemed unwilling to accept his apology. He tried to read but he was having trouble concentrating, and his breath smelled unpleasant and odd even with the throat lozenges on which he'd been bingeing.

In Reykjavík their group stuck together for a little while before heading to their various gates, and at a pop-up hair products store, Global Grooming, outside Blue Lagoon "Icelandic Skin Care Products from the Depths of the Earth," he bought some texturing wax while his buddies teased him about his relentlessness with the hair gel. The one he ended up with smelled mintier than he would have preferred and was expensive besides, but he bought it anyway. He tried seven different samples before he made his choice, and dropped each back into its rack. His friend Tom told him that this was the worst headache he had ever had, and Jussi kept coughing like a seal and wiping his face and dropping his handkerchief, grossing everyone out. They went into ELKO and horsed around hanging wireless Beats on each other's ears, and then settled on sandwiches and sushi at Mathús, appreciating the no-fuss self-service after having handled and rejected packaged pastas and curries and salads and two different cold soups. Jussi's connection was first, to Copenhagen, and Tom was off to London, and Willi to Frankfurt. Willem was staying in town overnight to meet some friends and then heading to Brussels, and Douglas was also going to London, and from there on to Bath.

All six, as they dawdled from one end of the Keflavík airport to the other, generated, with their sneezing and coughing and throat clearing, particle mists so fine that the microbe-laden aerosols could sail many hundreds of meters on the tiny air currents generated by the airport's air-conditioning system until they settled and stuck. Then they hitched rides on the next hands to come along and encounter those surfaces, as part of a microbial passenger list so teeming that the bacteria along for those rides outnumbered in each individual their total sum of human cells.

THE WORST THING EVER

A bunch of people had piled down the stairs of the cement wharf into a boat, but it looked like they were having trouble starting the outboard. They were pushing and shoving and arguing about it. One of the Villadsens went running past Aleq toward them. Out past the offshore rocks he could see tracks on some of the sea ice, bluer in the afternoon light.

Back at his grandparents' house, Hansenip from the next house over was standing at the foot of their bed. Aleq's grandmother when she saw him closed her eyes and warned him not to come too close. Under the covers she was wearing her blue sweater with the white stars. Mosquitoes lifted off and settled near her head. Hansenip told them that his wife had gotten sick two days earlier and this morning had sat down in their doorway and died. He'd gone to tell his in-laws and had found them dead in bed. He said that some of the sickest people were wandering the streets like they owned them, and that the Rosbachs were dead on two benches outside their house. His grandfather said to calm down, and that everyone should stay inside, and Hansenip answered that the one time you went out for what you needed, medicine or water or whatever, the sickness came back with you. His grandmother said they didn't want to give him their sickness, and he waved his hand in front of his face and told them he thought he already had it. He was crying and smoking, and they were crying along with him. Finally he said he should go check on his cousins, and they agreed with him.

Once he was gone they told Aleq again to keep back, but he sat as close as he could and got cold wet towels for their foreheads. It wasn't that he thought he could help, but he did think it'd be better to die before everyone else he cared about did. After he'd been there a while, his grandmother asked if he thought this was that COVID thing, and he told her what Miss Paarma had told him. She said she was thirsty and asked for some of her special water. She was talking about an iceberg stuck in the sea ice that they'd raided for freshwater all winter. She preferred tea made with it because she said the minty flavor brought out the taste of the tea. He asked his grandfather if he wanted another beer and his grandfather didn't answer, and his grandmother said no more beers for him because he'd thrown up the last one. She said what she always said about alcohol being most people's way of spoiling the occasion for others. Aleq could smell the throw-up on the other side of the bed once she'd mentioned it.

He sat there until it got dark. His grandmother was awake for stretches, but he didn't tell her about Malik. The cold towels he used on their foreheads felt a few minutes later like they'd come out of the oven. His grandmother pulled a hand out from under the blanket and felt his grandfather's forehead herself. They both shook the way dogs who'd been run too hard trembled in their sleep. His grand-father turned and hung over the side of the bed, and it reminded Aleq of a day they'd spent waiting out a seal's breathing hole, his grandfather bent over off to the side of the hole for an hour or more and not moving. His trick had been to rest a gull feather over the opening, and when the seal breathed out, the feather moved, and he had his shot.

THERE AND NOT THERE

During the night Aleq lay on top of the bed next to them because they were so hot under the covers. His grandmother called the name of the minister but she didn't say whether to try to get him. She told her relatives who were not in the settlement that she went to church but she usually didn't.

When he woke up again in the middle of the night he couldn't hear his grandfather breathing. His grandmother was breathing through her mouth like she kept being shocked by something. He turned on the light to see better, but he could barely look at her because he couldn't stand to see her in such pain. Her face was working at something, like she was trying to push her way through a crowd. She grabbed his hand, and squeezed it, and he told her that she'd done a good job of teaching him, and that he hadn't learned everything but he'd learned enough, and that she didn't need to worry.

"Why do you make that face?" his grandmother wanted to know.

"I smelled something," he said.

"What's the *matter* with you?" she asked.

"I'm sorry," he said. His eyes swam with tears. Why *was* he like this?

There was more wailing outside, out of nowhere, off in the distance. Lights were on all over the village, even as late as it was.

"What *is* that?" his grandmother asked, about the noise.

"Just some people," he told her.

"Tell them to shut up," she told him. "I'm tired of them." And she dropped her head back against her husband's, and breathed in three more times, and then stopped. Aleq waited, and then shook her hand where he was holding it. He shook it again. The noises outside stopped, too. He got up and turned off the light and sat back down with his grandmother and took her hand again. Now *he* was shaking, at being so alone.

Both their mouths were open. He let go of her hand, and lay on top of them, and kept them as warm as he could, and he finally fell asleep after it started to get lighter.

WOOD

He spent the next day in the house with his grandparents, mostly on the bed. Outside there was shouting, and calling, and the sound of more boats leaving, and then it was quiet.

The morning after that it was sunny. He went outside again. Old man Geisler was near his house and his son was facedown on top of the rocks. The Joelsens' mother was on her knees in a meltwater ditch with her hands out in front of her. Most of the dogs were tied up but a few had gotten loose and were trotting here and there and enraging the rest. One was digging holes and one kept rattling its long chains over the duckboards and rocks. In some places two or three people were piled together, and near Miss Paarma's house a gang of ravens had staked out one of the piles. Near the front door, ATVs and handcarts were parked at all angles.

He walked to his mother and father's house. They were on top of their bed together and he draped their blanket over their heads. Their feet stuck out. Their kids were all in their own beds.

At Malik's house Malik's mother was on her side in the kitchen. The baby was where she always was, on the mattress on the floor.

Down by the water a boy named Daavi he knew from school was shirtless and walking from house to house saying *Oh God Oh God Oh God*. Aleq headed down to the house he thought the boy had gone into, but he couldn't find him.

It was the older Villadsen's house. He used the bathroom and looked through the drawers and found pills and a jar of cream and a little pillow. In the kitchen there was a six-pack in the refrigerator and an egg and three blocks of cheese. When he came back outside, Villadsen's dog chained up across the way looked at him as though nothing interesting ever happened as far as it was concerned.

He was still wearing Malik's Nikes. He heard himself say, "I don't have any water." He didn't know who he was talking to.

He checked some other houses for Daavi and found him wedged into a corner of the Rosbachs' storage shed, panting and frantic. He shied away when Aleq leaned over him, and Aleq sat with him until he died. Then Aleq climbed up onto the shed roof, and from there onto the house roof, and sat with his elbows on his knees.

He felt like he hadn't slept in days, though he knew that wasn't true. After a while he got himself moving again, and climbed down, and walked over to Miss Paarma's house, and looked inside. She was on one of her beds beside two of her patients. She'd written names on pieces of paper and stapled them to people's shirts, but some weren't stapled right and when he opened the door they blew off the bodies.

At some houses there were notes on the front doors telling relatives to stay away. In some, people were wrapped in sheets, and, in one, a rug.

By the time the wind picked up even the dogs were getting quieter. In a lot of the houses the doors were open. Shirts and sheets flapped on the clotheslines. Miss Paarma's shed door kept squeaking and banging. He stepped where someone had burned some garbage near her water tank and it reminded him of his grandmother's saying that even if your yesterday was ashes, your tomorrow is still just more wood.

He slapped his face to stop staring at stuff and do something. It didn't feel like he'd live much longer but he also didn't feel sick. He started putting food he found outside where the dogs could get it. Some of the chained-up dogs were mean enough that he just threw what he had where they could reach it. He was dragging out a big bag of dog food and the Johansens' dogs were going crazy seeing it when he first heard the helicopter.

COUNTERTOPS AND PUMP
BOTTLES AND DOOR HANDLES

And credit cards and credit card readers and escalator railings and elevator buttons and phones and pens and water bottles and zippers and wineglasses and coffee cups. Yusef Zaki's nephew was getting married in Iceland and he wanted to be there and he'd convinced his girlfriend from Marseille to come along as well, and he stopped by Global Grooming out of boredom. Three American boys, Kenny Lee, Aaron Friedman, and Ben Stahl, heading home for spring break, considered upgrading their headphones before reminding themselves that there were no bargains at airports. A Chinese-Canadian family on their way to visit their son on his year abroad passed Jussi coughing and the father scolded him in Mandarin to cover his mouth. Five Scottish girls commandeered the miners' table at Mathús and one cleared away the unbussed trays and dishes before eating her carrots and hummus with her hands. A Swiss couple with a baby took the table after that. Two Austrian lawyers whose connecting flights had been delayed used the men's-room stalls after Christian and Willem. Anything the miners touched any number of people touched after them, and anything those people touched was available to any number of hands after that.

OLD RELATIONS NOT SEEN IN YEARS

Well before COVID-19, a survey in *Global Public Health* in 2006 had caused a stir in the international medical community by revealing that 90 percent of the epidemiologists polled predicted a major pandemic—one that would kill more than 150 million people—in one of the next two generations, because of the rapidly increasing number of candidate pathogens, the unaddressed shortcomings in global public health infrastructure and modes of cooperation, and the ongoing explosion of global travel, to name just three contributing factors. And perhaps under the heading of piling on was the discovery that the pathogen-recognition genes in our genomes are in some cases thirty million years old, which means those pathogens have survived among us long before we even evolved into the recognizably human, and so as our companions have been reliably causing cataclysmic epidemics not only for centuries, but for eons.

II

✦ ✦ ✦ ✦ ✦ ✦ ✦ ✦ ✦ ✦ ✦ ✦ ✦ ✦ ✦ ✦ ✦ ✦ ✦

Jeannine Dziri and Danice Torrone had had to get up so early for
their flight from Kangerlussaq to Ilulissat that they'd figured they
might as well stay up, and so they'd spent the three hours mostly
slumped blearily at the closed airport bar over a tiny curved counter
in their high-backed stools, checking and rechecking their to-do lists
and feeling sorry for themselves in minor ways before heading off
to their gate. Their tomato-red Air Greenland plane was making an
unscheduled early-morning departure, and though it had a capacity of thirty-nine, only five seats were occupied, and three of those
held their strapped-in cargo. Twenty-one hours earlier they'd each
been approached in their offices by their supervisors and told that
Greenland's Ministry of Health had granted permission for three
outside investigators to look into an outbreak that had apparently
spread from an eighty-person settlement on the western coast to a
town of five thousand, and while no one was clear on the situation
in the settlement, the town was already reporting at least eleven confirmed fatalities. The World Health Organization was sending its
communicable disease expert for northern Europe, and the Centers
for Disease Control and Prevention, Jeannine and Danice's supervisors informed them, was sending them. Danice would be the lab

wonk and doctor and Jeannine the epidemiologist, and their travel orders and flights were being arranged while they gathered as much information as they could from their supervisors and colleagues and what little briefing materials there were. They had four hours to go home, pack a bag, and get to the airport.

Jeannine was part of that year's class of new Epidemic Intelligence Service officers, and EIS officers were supposed to be on call twenty-four hours a day to respond to requests for CDC assistance with outbreaks or other public health emergencies. For her EIS assignment she'd chosen the Special Pathogens branch, partially for the anarchic appeal of its fighter pilot rep but also out of respect for the test pilot sensibility the work required: that Chuck Yeager–like unruffled absorption in the task at hand in situations in which anyone else would be freaking out. She'd been the center of every cocktail party conversation for a while following the COVID-19 pandemic. When she'd told Danice that her supervisor, who in cultural terms every so often seemed to reside in 1952, had merrily suggested that they call their pairing Team Estrogen, Danice had answered, "How about we call ourselves instead the Junior Certain Death Squad?" And Jeannine had laughed and told her that she might have scored the perfect partner.

FIRST THINGS FIRST

They didn't talk much on the first half of the flight. Danice looked like she could barely keep her eyes open. The idea was to go over everything you could find on the subject of the outbreak en route. There were lots of possibilities, from some kind of meningitis all the way down to any number of other things—including some kind of delayed mutation of COVID-19—but the place to start was probably with the case clusters that had already been identified at the hospital and the elementary school, and Jeannine needed to be ready to manage the way it was going to be all over the news and social media. She'd been warned that she could expect anything upon arrival, all the way from a hero's welcome to a version of "This is our investigation, so back off," but her first overriding communications objective after hitting the ground was to isolate the sick and quarantine anyone who was believed to have been exposed. Her supervisor had also reminded her that, as of their briefing, they were now attached at the cell phone, and that he wanted to hear from her whenever she needed resources, whenever she found herself in a political clusterfuck, whenever she had something he needed to hear, and even when she didn't.

She flipped through the journal articles and sample questionnaires and told herself every few minutes that she was just a small part of a very large team effort. And that every new position she'd ever taken had come with the same panicked questions: Was she prepared, and could she find the right people to help her out? And in each case she'd found her way. Whatever the urgency of the situation, she'd need to stay patient. A field investigation was never as clean as a research study, being way more poorly controlled, but the key would be avoiding something quick and dirty and pulling off the quick and clean instead. All she could do was take in what she could and then think for herself. They didn't know what the agent was or anything about its infectiousness, incubation period, lethality, or susceptibility to the usual containment measures. They didn't know if it could go airborne and, if so, whether it could travel meters or hundreds of meters. They did know that the worst news would be a person-to-person spread via the respiratory route, since adults took in about ten thousand liters of air per day and couldn't avoid inhaling each other's discharges. And Jeannine remembered reading somewhere about an outbreak of foot and mouth disease on the Isle of Wight that turned out to have been caused by a virus that had been windblown *fifty miles across the English Channel* from France without having lost its infectivity.

ALL THAT'S NEITHER HERE NOR THERE

What Jeannine *wasn't* thinking about, in her focus on the problem at hand, was the state of her private life, which, a month or so earlier by way of explanation for her behavior, she had described to her supervisor as two or three plane crashes beyond dire. During her postdoc she had through trial and error sussed out two discoveries—a way of driving boys wild with a tantric mix of kissing and touching, and a new method of targeting virulence traits without effecting the viability of the pathogens in her study—and she'd gone back and forth as to which had been the bigger breakthrough for some years afterward until she'd met Branislav when he'd been shoveling out an old man's car in a sleet storm. He'd dumped a load of snow on her legs and she'd teased him about it, and it had turned out that he didn't even know the old man. His hair later that night when she'd buried her face in it had smelled like bread and paprika, and the experience of certain of their kisses had never left her, like she'd harvested her happiness from them. Even in her Air Greenland seat she continued to touch her mouth as if she didn't know what to do with her lips. She had appreciated the way that first night his lack of hesitation had seemed to suggest *Why* couldn't *they be together?* and had appreciated even more the way, in the presence of their conversation, she had become as interesting and electric a person as she might have hoped.

All that had lasted ten months and had weathered easily the differences in their careers (he was a social worker), their backgrounds (his knowledge of Algerians was limited to the Pontecorvo movie and hers of Serbians to a recollection of some problems with the Croatians), and their families: his mother's central hope for him was that he would get back together with his ex for the sake of their child, and her mother once a week sent her links to articles with titles like "Why Are the Balkans So Violent?" under the subject heading "FYI." Ten months had allowed her to imagine that that kind of joy wasn't something that necessarily disappeared, and maybe *was* something that a woman could shelter inside indefinitely.

But little Mirko, Branislav's son, had been the kind of kid who'd turn over potted plants to see if the dirt would rain out or drop out in one big clump, and he never said much to her but his body language seemed to imply that things would improve if she took herself somewhere else. When she tried to show an interest he seemed automatically evasive, and she finally figured it was like the carcinogens you might pick up on a walk—you had to take the bad with the good—an attitude Branislav seemed to sense and resent. Most of his work was with at-risk kids and she had started a few conversations on the subject of how inept she was with children in general, and especially problem ones, and he'd always seemed unconvinced by her claims. He had arranged any number of times that she and Mirko could spend together, which she had watched the boy endure for his father's sake, and then a year ago on a return to the old country to meet his great-grandmother's relatives Mirko had spiked a fever of 104 and when the broad-spectrum antibiotics had had no effect he had died of sepsis in a hospital in Belgrade. It might have helped to have had the sepsis recognized before hospital arrival, but she had missed it. She was no MD but she *was* an epidemiologist and in the early stages she had been preoccupied with other things and had just missed it.

It took her weeks to figure out afterward that they now saw their relationship so differently that there were misunderstandings even where she most hoped for connection. Each time she told Branislav she loved him it had less effect, as if the notion had to be renovated to make it real to him. She spent longer periods in the shower, singing to no one. She'd been startled to find herself with someone who now seemed to experience desire as a weakness rather than a bond. He was dismissive of her need for him, as if it were dependence rather than what enabled her *in*dependence, and what he seemed to see as pride—as in, he wasn't going to pretend to something that wasn't real—she experienced as stinginess. Pleasing him felt like negotiating a box, and she started going into work like the local distributor when it came to sadness. For a week she thought of it as her own private form of civil disobedience before two of her coworkers at the lab she'd left for the CDC hauled her out of her chair and got her drunk and read her the riot act. It took a month after the breakup for her to realize that she was refusing to go anywhere that didn't have cell service on the off chance that he'd call, and after that revelation she found herself wondering if you were wrong to believe that you went on as yourself even after the loss of that person who had so decisively shaped you.

It was like she'd left the fast lane. It was like her days tiptoed around questions such as when she was going to clear the clothes he'd left from her closet. Everywhere she went it felt like someone had started to say something and then had decided not to. And then she told herself that she had to stop feeding this misery, and that she had to start to make getting past this a workaday routine. That she was thirty-four years old and there was no reason to stay so worked up. She needed to stop being ashamed of needing someone. People could need each other as much as they could manage. She needed to count her blessings. She had her legs, for example. And a good parking space at work.

And at least she'd *had* a relationship like that, Danice would have told her, if Jeannine had been the kind of coworker who opened up to people rather than sitting there like someone worried about a ringing in her ears.

Nearly everyone who had heard that Danice had become a lab wonk after having gotten her MD had annoyed her by remarking, "Well, *that* must be an interesting story." And in fact after every rotation in medical school Danice had been tempted to specialize in whatever she'd just encountered—obstetrics or hematology or whatever—but she'd gradually noticed that she kept staying interested in the bigger picture, and she'd ended up in public health, or, as she liked to put it, often on dates, as a medical detective. What she *didn't* say on dates was that she'd found she liked the solitary focus of the lab work more than dealing with patients, and after a few weeks in the CDC labs she'd realized that it was like being in the ICU, in that you were working with someone who could die without your help except that you were also trying to save all of those *other*, future patients that you initially had barely registered were out there.

Labs might have been the poor relation when it came to funding, but even so she ran a tight ship: every so often, for example, she liked to have her two techs prepare by hand the bacteriological and virological media that most labs ordered from catalogs, so that they weren't only sterilizing everything reusable but also were whipping up the gels and broths like someone starting out in a restaurant kitchen by chopping the vegetables. She informed her new arrivals that everyone in their line of work needed to be the obsessional type: the kind of shut-in who didn't throw away anything, especially those bits of data that didn't fit into their preconceived schemes of how something was supposed to operate.

She believed that, for better or worse, she'd acquired most of her drive from her mother, who liked to tell everyone that Danice's great-grandfather had started a paint company and her grandmother had run a travel agency out of her basement while raising four kids. The idea her mother was trying to convey was that Danice came from enterprising and adaptable stock. Her mother had also always asked her brother, once report cards were out, if those grades were really the best he could have done, and then after he answered would post Danice's report card somewhere where he could see it and follow her example.

The medical detective line had seemed to work pretty well on dates, but not much else had. She'd tried to make Jeannine feel better after Jeannine's one abbreviated account of her Branislav agony by joking that *her* most recent three relationships had all lasted from about one to five in the morning. She told Jeannine that one guy after sex had shown her a nude photo of his girlfriend on his phone, and another, when she'd been confiding in him how alone she felt, had asked if she'd seen his pocket comb. When she'd broken down about her loneliness to her mother on her last Thanksgiving visit, her mother had waited out her crying and then had reminded her pleasantly that boys had never been one of her talents. And when that hadn't helped, her mother had further suggested that she just think of loneliness as solitude with self-pity thrown in.

So Danice had gotten even better at embracing her inner perpetual motion machine. Even in a place where everyone worked long hours, she became used to that hush that followed once all of her coworkers had left the lab and everyone else's equipment was covered and the only sound, every so often, was another workaholic from some other department finally hitting the stairs. One dinner she spent with an old Slinky she'd rescued from a yard sale, toying with it next to her salad while trying to work out how it had ever functioned successfully as a child's toy. She wanted to be one of those people who remade the world she'd been handed, when it came to both her private and professional lives, but so far the world had not cooperated. When she was trying to rally in the face of that lack of success, she reminded herself that it was her job to just keep trying, and it was when her spirits took their inevitable dip that she remembered, in ways that seemed to sink her days, that that was her default position.

THE CONVERSION OF DROSS TO GOLD

They both dreamed of being John Snow, the nineteenth-century London doctor who had converted his nerdiness into heroism by being the first investigator to take the time to painstakingly plot on a map all of the known cases of cholera in his neighborhood, a stupefyingly labor-intensive strategy that inspired the simple recommendation that the authorities remove the handle of one centrally located water pump, thereby ending the outbreak.

CHAOS CENTRAL

At Ilulissat airport the hillsides were steep enough all around that the initial impression was that the runway had been dug out of the rock. The air traffic control tower was only two stories high and made the rest of the terminal look even smaller than it was. Inside the terminal, just behind a man holding up a sign for an adventure agency, a squat woman in a filthy parka was holding a sign that read "DR. DZIRI CDC!" "Think the exclamation point's a good or a bad sign?" Danice asked Jeannine. The woman introduced herself only as Doru, and after their bags were unloaded on a hilariously small baggage carousel that emerged from the wall near the door to the gate only to go back into the wall six feet later, she led them to an escort team waiting outside the terminal. The head of the team introduced himself as the translator assigned from the Ministry of Health and welcomed them to Greenland and said he hadn't realized the CDC was sending two women. He and his whole team looked Jeannine and Danice up and down with poorly disguised dismay, and he seemed further disappointed when he saw how little Jeannine and Danice had brought with them, even though Danice's portable lab, a cherry-red footlocker of high-impact plastic, was about five feet high. How much the weirdness with which they were being treated had to do with the darkness of Jeannine's skin was hard to gauge. Danice was being looked at the same way, mostly, but it also felt to Jeannine like there were differences.

It turned out that there were enough people in the welcome party that they'd need an extra small truck for the equipment, which they somehow hadn't anticipated, and that took a couple of glum phone calls from the escort leader to arrange.

Then, on the ride into town packed into a battered government van while they roared past long stretches of barren rock, Jeannine dealt with her anxiety by demoralizing herself with her overall to-do list: They had to confirm the outbreak and work on verifying the diagnosis. They had to construct a working case definition and record the case information. They had to develop some hypotheses and evaluate those hypotheses epidemiologically. They had to implement control and prevention measures and initiate and maintain surveillance. And they had to then try to communicate the relevant parts of whatever they'd found while managing a near-certain media shitstorm. She asked the head of the escort team where they'd be staying and he asked if she wanted to go there first to drop their bags and she said no, they'd better get started, as long as their bags would be safe in the van.

She asked if a quarantine had been instituted, and the head of the escort team said that they had done their best but they hadn't had the resources, and the parliament was convening tomorrow in an emergency session, and neither the airport nor the harbor had been closed to exiting traffic.

The road in from the airport wove south along the coast and the houses across the harbor alternated their colors—royal blue, pine green, brick red, taxi yellow—so aggressively that it looked like a children's book. The head of the escort team broke the silence twice more to ask Jeannine how long she had worked at the CDC, and both times she answered, "A while." Finally he tried Danice with the same question, and Danice told him, "Longer than *her*." The CDC prided itself on throwing raw recruits into the deep end of the pool, the theory being that this was the best way to learn. And also, her supervisor had joked, who *else* could be spared from the office for weeks at a time? The employee database had turned up one guy who spoke a little Danish who might have gone in her place, but he'd been sick himself when the call had come in.

At the hospital they could see so much chaos in the parking area outside the main entrance that they zipped themselves into their Tyvek suits right there in the courtyard, though the sight of them showing up looking like spacemen and sounding like Darth Vader would almost certainly cause more consternation. Until they knew better what was going on, they would be wearing their masks, and as the head of the escort team led them in, Danice reminded Jeannine not to kneel in anything because the liquid would soak right through, and Jeannine reminded Danice to make sure no hairs had broken the seal on her mask.

Once they were inside, some of the crowd shrank away from them and some milled around like they'd come bearing gifts. Some had tears in their eyes and one asked in English if Jeannine and Danice had come to take them away to safety. Jeannine asked a young woman in scrubs in front of them who was in charge, and she pointed to one middle-aged man and two younger men lying on cots in the hallway. She said that Dr. Kristensen was chief of medicine and Drs. Holm and Hammekin served under him. She said that Dr. Kristensen was holding on but had been unresponsive since early that morning. Dr. Hammekin was doing a little bit better.

Jeannine asked how many doctors they had on staff, and the woman answered six or seven, without explaining where the others were. When Danice asked if some of the others were available, the woman looked stricken and said she thought so but two hadn't responded to their pagers and the other one's pager was there on the counter. She introduced herself as Marie Louisa. She was the head nurse.

One of the other nurses took in Jeannine and Danice's interest in the men on the cots and said something caustic to Marie Louisa, and when Jeannine asked what she had said, Marie Louisa first looked embarrassed and then said that she'd complained that as far as the rich countries were concerned, the epidemic always began when the first white person got sick.

Some of the staff had clearly become even more alarmed by their suits, and Marie Louisa volunteered that the staff had no masks or goggles and had run out of surgical gloves and was now reusing their gowns and overshoes. The head of the escort team reassured her that all sorts of supplies were coming and said that many of them should have already arrived. Marie Louisa said that only two or three crates had. She seemed shell-shocked, and told Jeannine she usually gave out pills, condoms, and advice, and delivered babies and did minor operations and vaccinations and autopsies. When Jeannine had no response to that, the nurse added that the specialists like eye and ear people visited twice a summer and referred patients for extra treatment in Nuuk or Copenhagen. The same was true for dentists.

Jeannine and Danice complimented her on her English and asked if most of the doctors and nurses spoke English, and she said no.

She led them through the wards, which were chaotic. Everyone who wasn't inert looked terrified. She said there were fifty-one suspected cases and sixteen confirmed dead. They asked where the hospital had been keeping the bodies and she said they'd turned the maternity ward into a mortuary. She said that despite antipyretics the patients' fevers had stayed high, and the antibiotics hadn't worked, and the doctors hadn't gotten very far in their work-ups. The X-rays they'd taken had shown infiltrates in both lungs or sometimes even white-outs. The stages seemed to be coughing and lethargy and severe respiratory distress and confusion when speaking, and clearly the affected weren't getting enough oxygen, but intubations hadn't worked, and now three of the nurses who had performed the intubations were feverish and had developed their own coughs. Jeannine asked where the sick had been isolated and Marie Louisa pointed down the hall to a set of double doors with a bunch of homemade signs hung on them.

She led them into an office she identified as Dr. Kristensen's and showed them on a computer what she'd been able to compile, with help, so far, on the clinical features of the outbreak. The document went case by case, listing every patient by name, age, and gender, with their dates of hospitalization and treatments and outcomes.

Jeannine asked her when she'd found the time to do all of that, and Marie Louisa said mostly very late when the ward was quiet, and Jeannine said she was surprised it *got* quiet, even very late. Marie Louisa admitted that since this had happened, most nights it didn't, and Danice congratulated her on the quality of her work. Jeannine led Marie Louisa back out into the hallway and had her call for everyone's attention. When there was finally enough of a diminishment in the noise that a shouted voice could be heard, she had Marie Louisa translate for everyone that the CDC was here, and that she knew everyone was frightened of the epidemic and angry about the quarantine, but she and her colleague were going to help with both.

The head of the escort team seemed miffed that she hadn't asked him to do the translating. One of the medical staffers standing beside her put his face in his hands and said to himself what Jeannine assumed was something in Danish for "We're doomed."

THE NEW KEY IN AN OLD LOCK

On average the world encounters one new communicable disease each year, as pathogens evolve by leaps and bounds in ways that enhance their durability, transmissibility, and virulence: the keys to evolutionary success. What they're learning, through generations of trial and error, is how to work with their victims in order to work against them.

RING-A-LEVIO

The WHO communicable disease guy still hadn't arrived, and the head of the escort team didn't seem to know when he would. But all sorts of doctors were coming from Denmark, as well. And Jeannine immediately got on her cell to her supervisor, who agreed that until they knew what was going on, no one should be rushing in from other countries to try to help out, and that he would contact WHO to see if they could at least make sure of that. Jeannine and Danice took over a storeroom, and while Jeannine set up their laptops Danice unpacked the lab equipment the escort team had lugged in, including her TaqMan and GeneXpert systems. "Imagine?" she said as she unpacked them. "All this used to take up two rooms. Now it all fits in a check-in." "Isn't science amazing?" Jeannine asked, and Danice answered, "Aw, shut up."

One of the doctors who hadn't responded to his pager, a Dr. Olsen, had turned up and spoke some English. He said he was twenty-nine, he looked fifteen, and his specialty was obstetrics, but after they got him masked and gowned and eye-shielded, he was a much-needed extra pair of hands when it came to trying to keep all the patients under investigation corralled. He had very white eyebrows over what seemed like perpetually wary eyes, and something about the way he watched Jeannine made her self-conscious. The next step before examinations could even begin was to shore up the quarantine, and Jeannine had Olsen and Marie Louisa deputize six or seven of the bigger staff workers, even if they had no weapons to brandish. And while Olsen and Marie Louisa were addressing that group, which itself looked panicky enough to bolt, two teenage patients under investigation sprinted past the guard at the door and down the ramp, through the courtyard, and up the street. An older patient also tried to get out and had to be grappled back inside. It was like the Ring-a-Levio game from Jeannine's grammar school playground, when you tried to keep the kids you had captured rounded up while the other kids tried to break those kids out of jail, the result being a complete free-for-all.

They set up temporary negative pressure rooms for isolated patients, with a HEPA machine that discharged filtered air to the outside, and they set up a triage system in which the most febrile cases would be at the end farthest from the rest of the hospital, down the hall in the new surgery. Jeannine talked with Marie Louisa about what operators should tell people who were calling in, and how to go over the parameters for whoever was working the main entrance triaging new arrivals. In the meantime, some of the awaited supplies had rolled in, and everybody had new gloves and masks and eye guards and hair bonnets and that seemed to help a little. It also helped that the resupply had apparently involved cheese and beer. Everywhere you looked in the hallways, patients were sitting on the empty boxes that had been unpacked.

More antibiotics had arrived, as well, and with Olsen and Marie Louisa they worked their way through the quarantined patients, combining treatment with interviews. The notion that medicine was being handed out seemed to further help with some of the panic. That took most of the evening, and when it was over and most of the quarantined were sleeping wherever they could stretch out, the four of them convened to share information and to track on a big white-board who had reported what and when. Once they'd worked backward in time to the very first patient under investigation's reporting symptoms, it became clear that whatever this was, it had arrived on a boat with a guy who had come from Ilimanaq, a tiny settlement across the bay to the south. That guy had died the day before, and so had the two friends he'd stayed with. Even as late as it was, Jeannine had Marie Louisa try the health service nurse in Ilimanaq, and then the post office, as well, before she made some calls herself to arrange a helicopter from the Danish military for the following morning. When she asked Olsen if he could accompany them, he shrugged and gave her another wary look and said, "My morning's free."

A Danish news crew was now camped out in the courtyard, and had spent the evening shooting various exteriors and updates and otherwise killing time and waiting for the Americans to come out and provide some information beyond what everybody already knew. After Marie Louisa was thanked yet again and told to go get some rest, Jeannine headed out with Olsen and the leader of the escort team to meet with the crew to try to spread around some non-panic and at the same time take the opportunity to get some potential prevention messages out there. She took off her hood and mask before she got outside, to help with the non-panic part of things.

It was after three in the morning when she got back into their little office to collect Danice for the ride to where they were staying. Olsen had announced he'd be fine sleeping under the counter at the nurses' station. Danice had worked up some community surveys in addition to the work she'd done on the case definition. She'd also emailed some updates back to the CDC. They were both exhausted and frightened and didn't talk much beyond catching each other up. The hospital had quieted enough by that point that they could hear the delicate glass-breaking sound of ice collapsing off the gutters.

Danice needed to pack up, so Jeannine found a restroom and splashed her eyes and washed her face and did some stretches. They'd have time for about four hours of sleep before the helicopter was due to arrive. Jeannine wove her way past the sleepers in the hallway and stopped across from the maternity ward and peeked through the glass. She cupped her hands around her face to see better. Her eyes were so tired, it took them a long time to adjust.

The bodies were piled head to foot. Outside the window, in the gloaming of the not-quite-white night, a forklift was parked on the rock overlooking the harbor, along with two short rows of cargo containers. One of them was festooned with a bright roll of neon biohazard tape, as if constituting someone's idea of a mass grave.

THE DEAD ZONE

They met the helicopter at the airport, and the pilots were clearly disconcerted by the Tyvek suits and Olsen's full-body suit minus their breathing apparatus. One said, by way of introduction, that he liked to be addressed as "Pilot" rather than his given name. When Jeannine looked at him in response, he said he was just kidding. He then asked Olsen something in Danish, and Olsen gave him a noncommittal response. The copilot helped them load their equipment and there was a problem with the preflight checklist so the pilot had to shut the engine down and restart it. While they all waited, the copilot asked the women if their husbands were nervous for them, since they did such dangerous work. Danice said ironically that she was not a one-man girl, and the copilot, confused, said, "So you sleep around?," and Jeannine clarified that no, that wasn't what her colleague had meant. The pilot and copilot still looked puzzled, and Olsen looked worried and distracted, and then the pilot made a face and said that sleeping around was pretty much *all* he did.

The pilot asked Jeannine if it was hard for her in America, and she took him to mean because she was a dark-skinned Algerian, and answered that it was hard for a lot of people in a lot of places.

Then there was a twenty-minute delay because the pilot had been given orders only to set Jeannine and Danice and Olsen down in Ilimanaq and not to wait on the ground for them, and he complained up his chain of command while everyone waited. During a lull in the radio transmissions, Jeannine reminded him that they *had* to get to Ilimanaq, because they were doctors, and the pilot responded that from what he had heard, no one in Ilimanaq needed a doctor, because everyone in Ilimanaq was dead. Jeannine said that she doubted very much that whatever had happened there had been *that* dire, but her skepticism didn't seem to convince either of the pilots, so she finally made a call back to Atlanta. Her supervisor told her to sit tight, that he was all over it, and more calls were made while Olsen went off by himself and sat cross-legged on the ground with his chin on his fists. After another twenty-five minutes, someone got through to the pilots and yelled at them in Danish. They acknowledged the transmission unhappily and gave Jeannine and Danice some baleful looks, after which they rooted around in a plastic case in the cabin, donned masks and rubber gloves, handed their passengers headsets, and, finally, took off.

Once they had left the airport and the town behind them, they flew over a dazzling field of icebergs, some themselves the size of small towns. The pilot explained that this was the great Kangia Icefjord and then looked over his shoulder and seemed disappointed, though apparently unsurprised, at the women's lack of wonder in response. After ten minutes in the air at high speed, the dots of the settlement's houses in their primary colors appeared on the edge of the land ahead, scattered in their brightness across the huge rocks, but before they'd even made landfall, they could see bodies here and there on the rocks and the walkways and the grasses.

Over their headsets they could hear Olsen making all sorts of horrified sounds he didn't seem to be aware of. They did two passes over the settlement and saw lots more bodies but only some spooked dogs moving. *Are you kidding me?* Jeannine said to herself, and Danice, when they exchanged glances, looked equally stunned. They took off their headsets and pulled on their hoods and respirators. The copilot noticed and pointed it out to the pilot.

They came in low to set down beside the little lake at the settlement's helipad, a thirty-meter square laid out in the grass with rope anchored with buckets dug into the ground and loaded with rocks. To make it more official, there were orange hazard cones and a windsock.

The rotor wash disturbed the hoods and collars and sleeves of the bodies scattered nearby. On the other side of the lake, two more bodies were in the adjacent picnic area with its two tables, garbage can, and flagpole.

Jeannine and Danice and Olsen climbed out and unloaded their equipment. It took Jeannine a minute to adjust to the blinding quality of the light. The pilots stayed in their seats, saying nothing but looking like offended soccer players protesting a call. Olsen crouched over the nearest body while Jeannine and Danice divvied up what they'd have to carry and the dogs from the closest houses lunged and barked at them like they were defending the town. While all this was happening, the pilots' expressions were so exaggerated with resentment that Jeannine finally gestured that they could leave, and after some shouting to get them to understand that they should return in two hours the copter lifted off before she had finished speaking.

The women had to hunch over to steady themselves through the hurricane of rotor wash debris. Mostly because they were still stunned, they didn't move until some time after the helicopter was only a faint noise in the distance.

To their north they could hear the echoey yips and whoops of sled dog puppies. Jeannine resisted an immediate panicked call to Atlanta. They double-checked the seals on their gloves and masks. Danice hung her camera strap around her neck and slung everything else in her load onto her shoulders.

The three of them in single file tried to keep to the duckboards and wooden walkways because of the mud of the snowmelt. They had to step over a boy who was hanging off a walkway intersection beside an ATV frame that had been cannibalized for parts. There were a lot of flies and crows and ravens, and it looked like the dogs had taken an interest in some of the bodies as well. It was already hot in the Tyvek suits.

Jeannine unfolded the map with the health service nurse's house marked on it, and Danice helped her hold it steady and get her bearings, and then they headed toward it. The noise of the flies came and went with each body they passed. One of the dogs that had gotten loose tracked their progress but only kept up its barking halfheartedly.

They looked into every house along their way. Jeannine checked for anything useful, doing her best to adhere to that old axiom of field epidemiology when it came to the possibly relevant onsite clue: *Get it while you can.*

But it was impossible to maintain focus. In one house it looked like the whole family had died together. In another, the smell, even through his mask, made Olsen totter, and as they opened the entryway to the light Danice had to put a hand to her face shield.

While they checked subsequent houses, Olsen's face was streaming with tears he was unable to wipe away. Jeannine felt like she was still in a state of shock. Was there really no one here to treat? Were they looking at some kind of impossible mortality rate?

The nurse's house was a big red duplex with a plywood ramp up to the back door. They wove their way through a chaos of ATVs and homemade wagons out front and found her on one of the beds alongside some of her patients. Her head was black with flies. Other patients clogged the floor and the hallways and the other rooms. Some had their arms around each other.

There were big sheets of cardboard under all the shoes on the entryway floor. A Greenlandic flag was stuck in a little spray of dried flowers in a vase on the nurse's desk.

They brought her computer out of sleep mode and saw that some of her files were still open. They scrolled through them, waving away the flies, while Olsen translated. The woman had collected every piece of clinical data she could that might help someone understand what was happening, from medical histories with records of vital signs and the progression of symptoms to a catalog of throat swabs and blood samples and how they were marked in her refrigerator. Everything was there, waiting to be analyzed. There was still a big backlog of sent emails that hadn't gone out. They looked at each other in awe at what the woman had accomplished in the face of what she'd been confronting. And then Danice shrieked, almost giving Jeannine a heart attack, because there in the door behind them was a black-haired boy wearing a blue sweater with white stars and holding a full plastic bag to his chest, like that would keep him safe.

III

✢ ✢ ✢ ✢ ✢ ✢ ✢ ✢ ✢ ✢ ✢ ✢ ✢ ✢ ✢ ✢ ✢ ✢ ✢

III

Val's sister for her birthday the week before had given her a little homemade sampler, framed, with "Valerie Landry Is Always Late" stitched prettily in the center, so after Val tapped her ID on the reader at the parking lot gate at Rochester General, she texted, *Fourteen minutes early, Beeyatch*, and her sister texted something back, but then the gate was opening so Val wove her Prius between the buildings of the medical center, poking along with her windows open and imagining she could smell the landscaping. She only read her sister's answer when she was standing outside the glass-walled lobby that led to the ICU. On her way down the hall she nodded at all the worn-out men and women in green scrubs passing by at the end of their shifts. In her little office she hung her sweater on the hook on the back of the door and shrugged into her white coat and turned on her coffeemaker and woke up her computer. While she was waiting for her coffee she answered some emails. Her keyboard looked like it was nested in all the printouts and Post-it notes and eight thousand pens advertising labs or medications all over her desk.

When she was on her way to the department meeting for the shift handover, her sister texted again, and she silenced her phone. Two nurses at the nurses' station flirted in low voices behind their computer screens, and two interns around a crash cart were also murmuring, though it was clear they were arguing. The ICU quieted people, maybe because of the way it was set apart from the rest of the hospital, and everyone in it seemed to register that. Everything about it suited her, from the quiet to the importance of what she was doing to the combination of being needed and on your own, even if the latter could be scary. When she'd been an intern she'd even appreciated the way she could get a jolt of energy on some of the worst nights from just how worn down she was.

She'd always been one of those girls good at finding her own space and even better at doing what she wanted to do. In grammar school she'd been such a wool-gatherer that her teachers had decided it was never a good idea to send her on anything more than a two-step errand, and she'd spent a lot of her recess time reading, inside or out. Her hand was up so often in class that she supported one arm with the other, and by eighth grade it had gotten so bad that when she raised a hand her classmates lowered their foreheads to their desks.

She'd preferred neatness and order and girls at her table who didn't scream, and had been the school science whiz, an interest that when people asked she traced back to a homemade diorama of a Precambrian landscape that her father had found her in a junk shop. He had died when she was in ninth grade and she'd taken her biology final three days after the funeral and had gotten the highest grade in the class. Her mother had taken her father's death even harder than Val or her sister had, and while she had stayed funny and loving she had developed a smile like a shut door. They'd spent a lot of time afterward at her rich grandmother's house, which was so high on a hill they could watch storms passing by way off in the distance and never hear them, and there Val developed the kind of self-sufficiency that anyone left alone for long stretches in a big house would.

She'd become such a grind that all of those ordinary workaholics who passed up their one Sunday morning home with their kids to work out at the gym or take their weekly bike ride around Rochester had teased *her* about the way she was always looking to organize her dead time. When her current boyfriend had first informed her that he loved her, he'd registered her response and then had laughed and said, "Don't take it so hard." She'd always settled on guys like him, except for one night in med school when she'd off-roaded with a woman from her hematology class who'd stopped by for some notes and on her way out had taken Val's earlobe in her fingers and drawn her into a kiss. Val's current boyfriend told everyone who would listen that he'd immediately known he was crazy about her, and she always responded in those situations that she'd immediately known that she was fine with that. During her internship she'd hung around with a gaggle of wiseasses, especially one woman in pediatric oncology and another in gynecology who said she'd been pregnant during her residency and that the first noise her baby had recognized was the sound of her pager. So when Val's sister half-ironically texted things like *I feel like you're so distant from me*, Val texted back responses like *Who is this?*

INCOMING

At the handover both shifts gathered with their coffees and whoever was senior gave the rundown on each patient, spending a little more time on the new arrivals, and, if there were no other questions, at some point checked his or her watch and told everyone to get moving. On Val's way out of the meeting a nurse found her and told her that EMS had called into Emergency an hour ago with some incoming: two boys, nineteen and twenty, one six feet 160, another six-two 184, both with high fevers, both with severe respiratory distress, and those boys were being moved to ICU. They'd been stabilized and a few things had been eliminated but no one was sure about the diagnosis.

Whatever it was could be viral or bacterial or some kind of toxin but all the tests weren't back yet. And then *bam* the fire doors opened and the two rolling stretchers came rattling through, nurses scattering out of their way, and the ER resident caught Val up on everything that had been worked up so far and what they were still waiting on. At one point it sounded like he was seeing if he could speak only in abbreviations. The boys were Kenny Lee and Aaron Friedman and they'd been found in Aaron's parents' basement. One set of parents was here and the other was on the way. They hadn't found a wallet on Aaron but they had found a student meal card in his iPhone sleeve.

The nurses supervised the transfer to the beds and then ran lines and started up the monitors. Val checked Aaron's pulse, which panicked her a little, and even after the intubation he was breathing like he had a plastic bag over his head. Their temperatures came in at 104 and 104.5. Their lips were blue and their blood oxygen levels life-threateningly low, and the ABGs confirmed the oximeters. There was weird white stuff around the endotracheal tubes. The boys were further sedated and hooked to ventilators and rolled into prone positions, and the folders from Radiology that arrived displayed a rain forest of infiltrates in their lungs. Val's interns stood around looking baffled. They were on their two-week ICU rotation and had feared weird dire shit just like this. Val and the senior resident and the attending physician on call had just started talking about diuretics to deal with some of the fluid when first Aaron and then Kenny crashed. People went running to one bed and then when the alarms went off had to go running to the other. Everyone pitched in when it came to resuscitation, and Val was vaguely aware of frantic parents being herded away, and no one wanted to call it for either boy, but they tried everything, and nothing worked, and finally the senior resident who'd been running the code called it for Aaron and then moved over to help out at the other bed for a few more minutes before the attending called it for Kenny. After all the noise, there was a sudden relative quiet, and everyone stood around both beds and the chaos of the room and the tangle of the equipment, looking at one another in shock.

"Have we ever lost two people within a few minutes of one another before?" one of Val's internists, Ronnie, a string bean from Oklahoma, asked. One of the monitors kept beeping until someone shut it off, and nobody answered him.

THE FAMILY ROOM

Val dealt with Aaron's parents and the senior resident dealt with Kenny's. Val didn't do this very often, but when she had to, sometimes she took the loved ones into the Family Room and sometimes into her office. In this case the Family Room was closer, and the longer walk down the hallway before they heard the news seemed too sadistic.

She'd always been told that she needed to work on her bedside manner, but even having reminded herself, she couldn't stop wincing when she gave the parents the news. They had to be told twice. The mother, when she heard, stalled, like she'd been unplugged by the shock. The father turned and started walking along two walls of the room before ending up back in front of Val again. They demanded to know what had happened, and Val repeated to them that at this point what had killed Aaron wasn't clear, and the doctors were trying their best to figure that out, though they had ruled out some things. The father asked if it had been some new strain of coronavirus and Val said she didn't think so. The mother started keening and her husband pitched over to her and they grabbed each other in an end-of-the-world embrace.

Val gave them some time to themselves and washed her face and got some coffee. Then the mother came and found her and said she wanted to see the body. When they got to the room, the nurse who had just removed the tubes and lines slipped out. The mother put her mouth down by her boy's ear and told him that she was here with him, that he'd be okay, that she wasn't going anywhere. The father stood behind her. Val half turned away, moved, and was never clear on what to do with herself in such situations. The mother hung on to the bed rail and asked for a chair, and Val pulled one over for her and she sat, with a look on her face like she might recede to the end of the earth.

They all listened to the carts rolling back and forth down the hall. A distant wailing started that was probably the other mother. The father asked about Andrew and Abraham, and Val watched the mother realize that they still hadn't told Aaron's brothers, who turned out to be waiting in the lobby with a woman Val assumed was an aunt. The whole group gathered again in the Family Room, the youngest brother clearly already frightened by what he'd heard happening around the ward. The parents looked to Val to do the talking, and before she finished, the aunt cried out and the youngest brother stood up and walked out into the hall in a version of his father's response. The older brother put his hands on his ears with his elbows out like he was trying to muffle something deafening. Val gave them more time alone, and checked in with the attending, and then came back and stayed with them in a way that she hoped was supportive but unobtrusive, unpleasantly aware that she was about to add to their pain with questions.

The mother did most of the answering. It turned out that the boys had come back from their travels with the flu, and had planned to take it easy, but they'd gotten worse and worse and she'd found them both in front of the TV and called an ambulance. Where had they been? Prague, and Vienna, and maybe somewhere else; they'd talked about some side trips. She could check. Her husband handed her a Kleenex. And Val noticed that the mother's nose wasn't just running from her tears. Whatever he had, he gave it to us, the mother told her, making a face and pointing at the older brother.

The head critical care nurse informed her that Emergency had sent over another boy presenting with all the same symptoms, and though she was one of those nurses who was always putting her fists on her hips and acting like she alone was going to be able to handle whatever was hitting the fan, she looked as alarmed as Val at the news. Down the hall through the windows in the fire doors they could see a distraught man and woman flanking the reception desk. The nurse headed over to them to see what she could find out and Val took a breath and stuck her head into the room that was already a traffic jam of carts and people.

The new arrival turned out to be also nineteen, also tall, also in bad shape, and named Barry, and one internist asked him, "How're we doing, Barry?" though Barry was clearly in no shape to answer, and when the other internist hooking up the ventilator said about the white stuff surrounding the intubation "It's *sticky*," both internists looked to Val as the resident, and Val shrugged.

"Have you ever seen that before?" Ronnie asked.

"Not before today," Val told him.

Ronnie washed off his gloved hands like they were radioactive. This kid's numbers were a little better than the others' had been, and he seemed to be breathing a little more regularly, but given what had just happened the attending was going over him from head to toe, so Val backed off and figured she'd go do what she could for the parents.

They saw her coming through the double doors and took each other's hands. She tried to be lucid and to the point without being brutal: their son's condition was very serious, it wasn't clear what was causing it, and Val and her colleagues were doing all that they could. The mother looked at her like Val had kicked her in the face. She said that her Barry was a rare blood type; did they know that? Val thanked her for the information and asked if Barry was friends with a boy named Aaron Friedman or Kenny Lee, and the mother's face changed and she said yes, why? Barry had just seen those boys a few days ago.

By the time Val got back to Barry's room, the attending wasn't liking the way the boy's numbers were trending, and when she told him what she'd just heard, he said they had better call the infectious disease attending, and then asked if they even *had* an infectious disease attending. The one they'd had had taken a job elsewhere, and the attending hadn't heard whether he'd been replaced. They asked around, and the head critical care nurse said that the university had an infectious disease attending, and they made some calls and eventually heard that the guy had been pulled off the golf course and was on his way.

In the meantime he had told them that they should initiate the hospital's infectious disease protocols, and it turned out that there were three different sets that didn't completely agree. After some squabbling over that, the attending finally said, "C'mon, people, let's do what we can do, you know the drill," and everyone tied on masks and donned goggles and signs were made and hung outside Barry's room. Those who'd been in the room changed gloves and gowns.

With all that done, there was just the beeping of the monitors. The head critical care nurse said, "Do you think we need to think about a quarantine?" and the attending said that he'd just been considering that step, and then said that certainly anybody who'd been working with Barry shouldn't *go* anywhere. And one of the interns said, "What about his family?" And Val said, "What about everyone who worked on Aaron Friedman and Kenny Lee?"

Neither question seemed to be a popular one. Nurses fanned out in various directions, maybe looking for something that might be useful in a situation like this.

Val spotted a kid standing on tiptoe to see through one of the windows on the fire doors, just a pair of eyes and some messy hair, and said that for the time being they'd also better stop anyone from coming or going from the lobby as well, and the attending agreed, so Val picked up the phone at the nurses' station and told the front desk. The kid's eyes disappeared from the window.

She headed over to the window and looked through. Barry's mother was in a chair by the potted plant near the front doors, staring at her hands like they held the solution to her son's situation. Her husband had his hands in his pockets, and Val watched them both recognize Aaron's parents, still wrecked, who drifted over to them and hugged them. Barry's mother said something and then Aaron's mother said something back, and Barry's mother put her hand over her mouth.

The attending asked if anyone had an updated ETA on the infectious disease guy's arrival and a nurse said that he'd texted from the highway and by now he was probably only twenty minutes out. People were looking at their phones, and one of Val's interns kept asking if anyone had a signal. Outside, a thunderstorm had hit, and with every lightning flash in the darkness, it looked like the parking lot with its berms and trees reappeared and then vanished.

Val had two texts on her phone, one a GIF from her sister and one in which her mother complained that if she was catching another cold she was going to kill herself. She texted both of them, *Another slow day in the ICU*, and texted her boyfriend, *Might be stuck here a while after my shift*, and then ignored his immediate *What's going on?*

A half hour after that, the infectious disease guy still hadn't arrived and Barry crashed, and they couldn't save him. Coming out of Barry's room, the attending didn't look overwhelmed, but he didn't look composed, either, and given that he was usually all about calm, whenever he seemed anything else everyone tended to get petrified. He maintained a we-got-this expression on his face that even in its inauthenticity was probably more persuasive than Val's. The infectious disease attending strode in and said, "Where's the patient?,"

and then saw everybody's faces and immediately sobered up. He spent some time in Barry's room, and when he came out he conferred with Val and the attending, and then examined Aaron and Kenny. When he finished that, he started making calls.

"Any ideas?" the attending asked, and the infectious disease guy, holding the phone, said, "Not yet," and then changed his voice when he got through to whoever he was calling, and gave a rundown of what might be going on, including a potential need to initiate a lockdown on the ICU.

One of the interns still didn't believe what was possibly unfolding. Val could see it in her eyes: it was like when you passed a highway accident and then spotted all of those oncoming cars still heading toward it, unaware.

The thunderstorm, meanwhile, was still going. Val found her snack in the fridge and slid her mask off and sat for a minute, eating pita wedges and celery from a baggie, and tried to get ahold of herself.

Her courage was starting to feel slippery, like something she needed to pin down, and between deep breaths it felt like she'd startled an animal in her rib cage. She told herself with impatience that it was time to be what she'd been pretending to be, and she slid her mask back on and stood up to get back into the game.

The infectious disease guy was asking for a list of anyone who'd had any contact at all with any of the three boys, or who'd had contact with someone who'd had contact with them, and Val's intern from Oklahoma said, "Well, that's pretty much everybody," and Val smiled at him, like, *Well, you've got us there.* And then to get herself going, she poked her head into one of the other rooms, where a forgotten patient sat wet-eyed and silent, and she asked if he was all right, and then when he didn't answer she told him to sit tight, that someone else would be by before too long.

IV

✣ ✣ ✣ ✣ ✣ ✣ ✣╬✣ ✣ ✣ ✣ ✣ ✣ ✣ ✣ ✣ ✣ ✣

At Danice's shriek the kid bolted, and Jeannine and Danice just stood there, staring, but Olsen took off after him. He slipped on the plastic bag the kid had dropped in the doorway and did what looked like a painful split, but by the time Jeannine and Danice got themselves outside he was just a few feet behind the kid, and at a turn near a little bridge over a brook he took him down. A few dogs still chained nearby scattered and barked.

The kid fought and kicked and Olsen's eyewear and mask were knocked askew but he righted them and then heaved himself on top of the kid's legs and back and pinned him into some spongy grasses and thistle. The dogs yelped and gyrated on their chains and one broke free and charged at them and then dodged away.

The plastic bag had some cheese and an egg in it. Jeannine held it open for Danice and then they both hustled over to Olsen and the kid. Olsen was talking to him in Danish and the kid had stopped struggling. He lay there, quiet, and they all waited until he finally answered, and when he was finished talking, Olsen reported that his name was Aleq, and that he didn't think he was sick, and that he also didn't think that anyone else was still alive.

Aleq had hair like Branislav's son, Mirko, and Jeannine was a little startled that her mind had made that connection. His nose was running, and also like Mirko you could see on his sleeve where he was always wiping it. She told Olsen to tell him that they needed to examine him and to ask if he was going to be okay if they let him up. Olsen conveyed all of that and then waited, but the kid didn't answer. He was looking through the grass off into the distance and his eyes were full of tears. Jeannine crouched nearer to him so he could see her face better through the clear plastic hood, and Danice did the same. At first he didn't glance over at them, and Jeannine could feel the sweat on her back from their suits in the sun. Then he gave them a look and said a few things, one after the other. When Olsen stayed silent, Danice finally said, "Well?" Olsen cleared his throat and then reported that the kid wanted to know if they could help him bury his grandmother and grandfather. And his friend. And his parents, and their kids.

Since she couldn't reach her eyes Jeannine had to blink energetically to clear them, and she could see that Danice was doing the same. She told Olsen to tell Aleq that yes, they could help him, but first they needed to make sure he was okay, and then they needed to check for any other survivors.

Danice asked Olsen if he'd hurt himself when he'd slipped, and Olsen said no, but he winced when he said it, and Jeannine imagined that his reaction was about having had the kid's foot in his face and his mask knocked off. She winced herself.

They did their examination in one of the houses they'd found empty on their way to the nurse's house. On a kitchen table they'd cleared for him they took his temperature and checked his blood oxygen. He didn't want to sit still for any of it, and he and Olsen seemed to be increasingly annoying each another, though when Jeannine asked about it Olsen shook his head and told her she wouldn't understand. "Maybe it's a colonial thing," Danice suggested, and Olsen told her sharply that it wasn't a *colonial* thing.

The boy kept his eyes on Jeannine while she was asking questions and even while Olsen was translating. He told them he hadn't thrown up the way the others had. He hadn't been shaking the way the others had. He hadn't been so sweaty he'd soaked through his clothes the way the others had. He answered each of Olsen's follow-up questions from Jeannine as if impatient to get off the table. He hadn't had a cough. He hadn't had trouble breathing. He *had* had a runny nose, and a sore throat, and he'd gotten them the same time his friend Malik had gotten his. Malik had then gotten all of those other things. And Malik had been the first one to get sick. When he threw that out there, Jeannine and Danice exchanged rapid looks, and then Jeannine started firing so many questions at him that both he and Olsen looked taken aback.

When had they gotten sick? What had they been doing just before they got sick? Had they been near any animals? Had they been anywhere they had never been before? The barrage caused the boy to shut down, and all of her attempts to get Olsen to follow up with him got nowhere.

They didn't have much more time before the copter would be back, so Jeannine proposed that Danice stay behind with the boy and that she and Olsen check out the rest of the settlement for survivors, but as they started to leave the boy cried out, and when Jeannine looked at Olsen, he explained with some surprise that the boy had said that he wanted the dark-skinned one to stay with him. "I can't catch a break even with the twelve-year-olds," Danice said, and Jeannine, after a moment, said, "It's fine with me if it's fine with you," and Danice said, "I can handle it," and she and Olsen left.

After they were gone, the boy slid off the table and slumped in a chair near the window. She could see he was trying to hold it together, but then the tears ran from his eyes and nose and his body shook so much that his chair legs rattled on the floor. He retrieved the ratty sweater they'd removed to examine him and draped it over his shoulders, though it was hot in the room, but it kept slipping off, and finally she stepped forward and tucked the sleeves around his neck to help it stay.

He said something she assumed was thank you. Some ravens cawed outside. He wiped his nose again and she put the outside of her gloved hand against his cheek, and for a moment he closed his eyes and leaned into it, and then he swayed back upright. He wiped his face and then flexed his dirty fingers in front of it like he was vaguely amazed at the intricacy of a human hand.

That pained I-don't-quite-see-you absorption in something else also reminded her of Mirko. In the morning he would set up his trains on the hardwood floor beside his father's bed and she'd have to step over both them and him on her way to the shower.

"I think you may have known our index patient, Mr. Aleq," she told the boy, and he looked at her as if in response, and then looked out the window. "There's a whole lot of information we likely need to pull out of you," she added. Then she leaned forward to see, out the window, what had his attention.

A few sled dogs were sitting and standing in front of the house across the way, looking back at her. The closest had lost an eye and was staring over with its remaining one. It was hunched in a plywood box set on its side that its owner had dug into the turf as a doghouse.

They'd need to examine a lot more closely where this boy had been living, and his friend's house as well, as well as whatever bodies were still in either, and they also needed to bring away a lot of material from the health service nurse's house. If there really were no other survivors maybe they could leave Danice to begin all of that while Jeannine and Olsen got the boy back to the hospital. Then they could collect everything else, including what Jeannine would have to explain to the pilots were potentially extremely dangerous throat swabs and blood samples, in a second load. So the next hurdle once the pilots got back was to talk them into ferrying both the kid and then the materials. The kid would be in the portable isolation chamber—the ISO-POD—that they'd stowed in the copter's cargo compartment, so maybe the pilots would be okay with that. And maybe in terms of the other materials she could reassure them about the way she'd packed and sealed everything, and about Danice's expertise with travel protocols.

"Maybe I can flap my arms and fly to the moon," she muttered to herself. And when she looked over, Aleq had returned his attention to her, like even *he* was glad he wasn't in her shoes.

Meanwhile the clock was ticking and there was no internet here on this rock so she had no way of knowing whether things were getting more or less out of control back in Ilulissat.

While she waited for Danice and Olsen to return, she had Aleq stand, and she gowned and gloved and masked him to inhibit the spread of infectious particles from his clothing and hands. He didn't seem to need to have explained to him what she was up to, and he stood patiently throughout all she was doing. Before she finished zipping him up, she redraped his sweater over his shoulders and loosely tied the sleeves again under his chin, and he seemed to appreciate the gesture.

When Danice and Olsen finally returned, they both were streaming with sweat inside their suits, especially Danice, and it was hard to tell who was the more shaken up.

"It just seems impossible that it would be *everyone*," Danice told her. Olsen didn't say anything, and looked even grimmer than he had before. Jeannine outlined her plan for taking Aleq back and leaving Danice behind alone, and Danice seemed less than happy with the idea, but game. She rested a while in the shade of one of the houses, and then separated out the equipment she'd need from what Jeannine would be taking back with her.

Then it was Aleq's turn to hear the plan, through Olsen, and he shook his head violently and accused Jeannine of something, and

Olsen translated that she had promised to help him with the burials. She instructed Olsen to reassure him, promising that his family and friend would be taken care of, but there were other things that had to happen first, and they needed to take care of both him and other very, very sick people in Ilulissat. They went back and forth about it until the boy finally quit, looking so stricken in his helplessness and his oversized gown and mask that her heart went out to him even more than it already had.

They all stood around him sympathetically until Olsen finally told them that he could hear the copter returning in the distance. Jeannine told Danice that they'd better get the ISO-POD together, and Danice gave Aleq one more look before complying. "I'd say he's holding up pretty well for someone who's watched everyone he knows kick the bucket," she said.

Olsen asked what "kick the bucket" meant, and Danice told him. He gave her another one of his wary looks, like he wasn't sure whether or not she was telling him the truth.

"They have a saying," he finally responded. " 'The wolf keeps the caribou strong.' "

The ISO-POD's carry sack had "AIRBOSS DEFENSE ADVAN-TAGE" printed across the top. They unrolled and inflated it on top of a spinal board on the duckboards outside, since there was no gurney, and by then the copter was so close even Jeannine and Danice could hear it through their hoods. After it set down inside the hazard cones near the windsock, they had Aleq get down on his butt and slide himself into the ISO-POD carefully, feet first, and once they'd sealed him inside and turned on the air, they wiped the outside down with antimicrobial wipes. He seemed distressed by the white noise of the blower motor. It was loud enough that Olsen gave up trying to shout reassurances through the vinyl. On Jeannine's count they hefted him up using the board's handles, Jeannine and Danice on one end and Olsen on the other, and then they lugged him along the duckboards to the landing site. Even in the short while they had the apparatus in the sun, they could see that it was starting to act like a greenhouse for the poor kid.

"What *is* that?" the pilot asked them, in English, when they arrived, and Jeannine explained calmly that it was a mobile transport system, a collapsible vinyl enclosure that created a negative pressure environment for more safely transporting potentially infectious patients.

The pilot and copilot said nothing in response, but provided no help in sliding the apparatus in across the copter's rear seating area. Once it was in and secured, Jeannine and then Olsen climbed in awkwardly around it, spreading their legs and setting their feet wherever they could for the ride. The copilot slammed the rear doors shut, and Danice gave them a parodic, last-girl-on-the-*Titanic* cupped hand wave as they lifted off.

A SMILE EXPLAINS EVERYTHING

In the hospital Aleq sat on the bed under the sheet that they'd thrown into the thing they'd carried him in, after the guy who spoke Danish had told him to take off all of the stuff they had put on him, and his clothes, too, as best he could in the narrow space, and then they'd given him another long shirt that went down to his knees. The tent was very small and he could see through all parts of it, and there were plastic sleeves that drooped over him on both sides that they stuck their arms in every so often. He could just about sit up before he hit his head, but the whole thing was soft and smelled like the waterproof covers people used around the settlement. The doctors and nurses all wore masks and gloves, including the two in the space suits, and they had another clear sheet of plastic across the door to his room. Through its cloudiness across the hall he could see nurses and doctors coming and going from around a crib. The sickness wasn't there in his bed yet, but he assumed that it was on its way, gliding toward him. When he leaned over he could see open and closed doors farther down the corridor, and knew that the Greenlandic patients didn't want to be alone, so any closed doors meant there was a Dane in that room. He imagined all those sick kids at night like Malik, opening their eyes in the darkness.

The tent made a lot of noise that sounded like rushing water and was so loud that he had felt more than heard the thumping blades over his head on the helicopter ride. He hadn't been able to see what they'd been passing except for the occasional top of an iceberg until they'd tilted to turn, and he'd caught a glimpse of the twinkling lights of the container terminals. On a second turn he'd recognized the bay they called Some Fish Sometimes, and then he hadn't seen anything more until they'd lifted him out after they'd landed.

The dark-skinned woman with the space suit slid her arms into the plastic sleeves and the Dane who did all the talking told him that they needed to take some blood, and the woman said something else and the Dane asked if Aleq was afraid of needles, and Aleq said no, and the woman smiled. He imagined that she smelled like medicine and coffee.

He asked what her name was, and she told the Dane, and the Dane told him. He had trouble saying it, and she tried to give him some help but he couldn't hear her.

She said something else in a low voice and the Dane asked Aleq again if he and Malik had been anywhere or come across anything unusual before Malik got sick. The edge of the pit at the mine bobbed up into Aleq's head, along with the smell of the cold air coming up from below, and the smell of the rock after that. He felt guiltier but wasn't sure why, and rolled onto his side so he was turned to face the wall and could stop thinking about it.

They left him alone for a while and he dozed, and when he woke he started remembering again. He managed to get Malik out of his head but not his grandmother, and he remembered that when he was little and bothered her, she always said that she had clothes to mend and harnesses to repair and food to make but she still found time to sit on the floor with him and play his games. Sometimes she'd set him on the counter and say, "Aren't you ugly? Don't I have the ugliest little boy in the whole settlement?" and he'd answer, "*You're* the one who's ugly. It must be hard for people to share food with you." Some mornings they just stood at the kitchen window and looked down at the water. When he had tantrums she picked him up and carried him around the room until he stopped. When he made too much noise in the early mornings she always asked if someone had hired him to come keep her awake. When he was older and went on about something she thought was stupid, she would listen for a while and then finally tell him to get some water for the pot, or his bath. She embarrassed him with the way even when there was a big line at the grocery store she would pick through each egg carton and lift out and inspect every egg. And with the way she eavesdropped on arguments or bad behavior. When he complained about it, she told him that when there was a real quarrel it was better than a movie. He had also been impatient with how much she talked about her cousins, who had moved to Ilulissat and sold seabird meat from the trunk of their car or laid out on cardboard in front of the supermarket.

When she'd had wine, she liked to talk about the competitions the catechists had arranged when she was a girl in school, and the way she won them almost every time, because you had to learn a piece of scripture and recite it without mistakes, and she was good at it, maybe because she just liked remembering the sounds. She also talked about her childhood in Eqi and waking up in winter and the way her mother would let her and her sisters stay under the quilt until the cabin warmed up. Once their father had had his coffee, the kids would get their tea and rye bread, and on the coldest mornings they got to eat under the quilt.

He must have slept, because he woke up alone and panicked before the dark-skinned woman came in to see him. An older nurse came in with her and the nurse asked him if he felt all right and after talking with the woman asked some other questions too. The woman put down what he answered in a little computer.

He asked what had happened to the Danish doctor, and her expression changed, and she said something to the nurse and the nurse told him that Dr. Olsen had gotten sick.

Something was occurring to him and it took him a while to bring himself to say it. "Am I making other people sick?" he asked the nurse, and she had to lean forward to hear him through the plastic, so he asked it again in a much louder voice.

She said something to the dark-skinned woman and the woman waited, and then said something back, and the nurse told him that they weren't sure about that, but they were trying to find out.

He asked if Dr. Olsen was okay and the nurse didn't want to answer at first and then finally said that no, he was very sick.

"Did I make Malik sick?" he wanted to know. "Did I make my grandparents sick?" The nurse shushed him, and tried to pat his arms with hers in the plastic sleeves.

"Did I make everyone sick?" he wanted to know, but even as he said it he already knew.

"We're not sure who made who sick," the nurse told him, but he yelled at everyone to get out of the room, and tried to tear the seam of his tent open, and the woman and the nurse held him down and called for help and other people came in and helped hold him down, three on each side, and one of them gave him another shot.

It took him a while to calm down, and he could see how much the other people who'd been called in didn't want to be near him.

At some point he stopped yelling, and had trouble keeping his eyes open, and one by one the other people left. Finally it was just him and the dark-skinned woman.

His arms felt like they were floating. He told her that, but he knew she didn't understand. She didn't seem impatient sitting with him, and his head was filling with a white mist, and the two things together made him feel generous, like he wanted to give her something back. He also liked her because the first time she'd crouched near him and caught his eye, she'd surprised him with her smile, and it had made him think about the time he'd complained to his grandmother that one of these days her eavesdropping on other families' fights was going to get them into trouble, and the way his grandmother had shrugged and told him that a smile explained everything.

He put his hand up toward the woman, against the plastic, and she gave him another, smaller, smile, and called the nurse back into the room. The nurse asked if he was feeling better, and talked to the woman for a little while, and then asked him more questions, and he knew that they just wanted help, and he wanted to answer, but he didn't.

The woman said something else to the nurse, and the nurse told him that the doctor wanted to know what his friend had been like. He didn't answer that, either.

The two of them finished what they were doing and put some of what they were working on away, and the woman nodded toward him and said something else, and the nurse shrugged. The nurse said to Aleq, "She wants to know if you're ever going to talk to her, or whether she should just stop bothering you."

Malik had always complained that when he hung out with Aleq he had to do all the talking. Malik had told him once that a cousin had said he wanted to move to their settlement, for the quiet. And when Aleq as usual still hadn't said anything back, Malik had added, "He's going to like talking to you."

So Aleq cleared his throat and decided he would say something. He told the woman that his friend's name was Malik, and that Malik always told people about him that if you answered Aleq's first question you just got two more anyway. Both women looked surprised, and after the nurse told the dark-skinned woman what he'd said, the dark-skinned woman laughed. Aleq told the nurse to also tell her that Malik last summer had run away from home for two days and had lived under a big rock near the shore off the road to Qasigiannguit on fish and two boxes of crackers, though his mother had known where he was the whole time.

The dark-skinned woman looked like she didn't know what to say to that. When she finally did answer, the nurse said that the doctor thought that it sounded like he and Malik were quite the explorers, and once the nurse explained what that meant, he told her that yes, they did go all over the place, and he told her some of the places they'd been.

When the floating went away, later, he screamed at them again, but he was really screaming at himself. They gave him more of whatever they had given him before to calm down, and it made him feel more lenient toward himself, though he saw what he was up to. It was like the way everyone said that bad fishermen blamed their nets for having holes. And once they'd left him alone in the dark, though the floating kept him from getting too stirred up about it, it was like he was hanging Malik and his grandmother's pictures in his head where he could see them, the way his grandfather set out his cod net in the sun. And in the middle of the night when the floating went away again, it was a shock, like the time he'd broken through thin ice and had felt the jolt of the cold as he'd seen underwater the floating wings of his open anorak above his boots.

Sometimes he wasn't aware he was crying until they came in to help him. The floating made it easier to be alone. Without it, he had to face that he was nowhere and with no one, like the night he'd been helping out in his grandfather's boat offshore, and the black line of their settlement, with all the lights out, had suddenly looked like a place he'd never been. Without the floating it was like how he'd felt on his grandparents' bed the morning after they'd died, when he couldn't hear a single voice or noise outside and had wondered if even the dogs were dead.

When he was very little, Malik had told him that the one grave all by itself out near the rubbish dump was for a qivitoq, and had dared him to go sit on it. That Sunday, Aleq had asked the minister why the qivitoq had been buried there, and the minister had told him that it was because the qivitoq, when he'd been a man, had taken his own life and couldn't be buried in the cemetery; he had to be buried by himself. But he could have a cross, because he'd been baptized as a baby. And when Aleq had asked why the stone mound over the body was so big, the minister had told him that with a qivitoq it always had to be three times the usual size, to keep him from getting up.

He figured out that squeezing his eyes shut helped him clear his head, especially late at night. He reminded himself that some of the settlement's best hunters had been orphans, like old man Hansenip, who everyone said had been so full of lice as a kid that families had only let him sleep in their mudrooms, and who had always had to steal his meat from the smaller dogs. He told himself that every day he took care of himself, it would make him less afraid. He told himself that it was like the old saying that everyone had to do his own growing, however tall his parents had been. He remembered his grandmother's always reminding him that the quickest way to find out what you really needed was to go without.

But even after all that, some nights he woke up crying loud enough that the nurse and the dark-skinned woman turned on the lights when they came into his room. He told the woman that his eyes wouldn't stay shut. He didn't tell her about the night he spent dreaming he was a stone. After a few nights of his crying, she wheeled a bed on a table in next to him and lay down on it herself, and turned off the lights. After that he slept better.

Though when he woke, for some reason he remembered the morning his grandmother had brought him to see his parents' new baby, and how he'd stood there in this house he didn't live in, unsure what to do, while his grandmother had touched her coffee cup to the baby's lips and then had held some seal meat and potato and boiled onion up to its nose before she'd said to it, "This is your brother," and had turned its little body to face him.

V

✧ ✧ ✧ ✧ ✧ ✧ ✛ ✧ ✧ ✧ ✧ ✧ ✧ ✧ ✧ ✧ ✧ ✧

Just when she thought she was getting somewhere with the boy he shut up again like a clam. She was rapidly feeling both that she didn't have time for this and that he was in some ways the key to everything. Olsen's having gotten sick had panicked everyone, and nothing they were trying with him looked like it was helping. Meanwhile Danice's TaqMan, a multipathogen assay that tested for forty-eight different pathogens, had come up with nothing, and neither had her GeneXpert. They were target-specific probes, and whatever it was, as she put it grimly, it apparently wasn't on the list. Between the samples from the ward and what Danice had brought back from Ilimanaq, she figured she'd been averaging eighty tests a day. She'd also already shipped some 130 samples back to the CDC. Jeannine reminded her that even negative results at least tended to reduce the spectrum of possibilities, and that the wonks in Atlanta had started to design newer assays that were even more generalized, and they had hopes for those. They also thought they were starting to figure out the incubation period, roughly, and had found in most of the survivors IgM antibodies, the kind the immune system produced when it recognized that it had never encountered a particular disease before. Danice had taken to calling what they were dealing with the

Churchill Bug, and when Jeannine had asked why, she'd said, "You know, that Churchill quote about Russia being a riddle wrapped up in a mystery inside an enigma."

Any number of Level 4 labs were now working with specimens, but most of the newer methodologies like PCR to screen for recognizable fragments of DNA or RNA were good only for searching for what was familiar or very similar to something familiar. But for something new you couldn't locate its signature if you didn't know what the signature was. Given PCR's limitations, then, the alternative was to sequence whole genomes, and if they'd had a candidate pathogen they could have done so, but without one all they could do was take samples from the victims and look for things that would indicate the presence of a virus or bacterium or whatever. They were even back to the old-school approach of trying to grow the thing in a cell culture and then just looking for damage.

Danice caught Jeannine up on the latest emails while they both examined Olsen. Only Level 4 biosafety labs were cleared to work on this thing now, given how dangerous it was, and various teams had been offering whatever was in the samples various cell lines known to be hospitable to respiratory pathogens, without success. Though they'd just started working on it. Mostly there'd been a lot of groping. Danice said that so far it was like trying to find bats on a moonless night by listening.

"I can't tell you how reassuring that is," Olsen told them from where he was lying, and Jeannine and Danice looked at each other with chagrin and then worked silently for a few minutes, before Danice eventually went on.

Columbia's School of Public Health had been pulled into it with their supposedly cutting-edge molecular diagnostic systems like high-throughput sequencing and MassTag and GreeneChip, which could screen for thousands of known pathogens simultaneously, and they'd come up empty so far as well. Given that many of the symptoms resembled a bizarrely lethal pneumonia, everyone had thought of anthrax, an old standby, since the rule of thumb was that if you heard hoofbeats and you weren't in Africa, it was more likely a plain old horse than a zebra. And the whole thing *presented* like a bacterial infection, followed by a whole lot of cell death. But then where was the bacteria?

By day three of Olsen's infection, his blood oxygen levels were so low that Marie Louisa kept rapping her oximeter on the table and reapplying it, and he didn't take well to encouragement. She kept tearing up with a brave smile when she caught his eye, but she finally stopped and left the room after he shouted at her about it.

Even as sick as he was, he was beside himself that he'd made his little girl sick, and he swore that he had come in as soon as he'd started feeling at all ill. It had been so *stupid* of him to have gone home at all, he said. What had made him think he could go home?

"We shouldn't have let you," Jeannine told him. "It's as much our fault as yours."

The look he gave her in response was filled with so much fury it shut her up.

She stopped trying to make him feel better about it, beyond reminding him again that he had come in as soon as he'd started feeling sick.

Which was a bad sign when it came to the other big question, which was whether the symptoms appeared before or after the patient became infectious. Symptoms first was much less dangerous, since sick people could then decide not to go out, or be quarantined. With pathogens like the flu, though, high infectivity *preceded* the symptoms. That had been the case with COVID, too; you got other people sick, and *then* you felt sick. And it was starting to look like this pathogen operated the same way.

Jeannine's insomnia meant that once Danice finally conked out she spent more time with the boy. She was impressed with the way it felt like in the middle of the night with everything quiet he was resisting with his impassivity the universe's indifference to him. He seemed to gather strength from the improbability of his survival. Instead of sleeping, he looked like he was cycling back through unhappy memories, and she knew how that worked.

Every so often she registered the number of new cases even in just their ward and caught a glimpse of the full scope of what they were up against.

Identifying it was only step one. Step two was finding out where it had been all this time, and step three why it had emerged where and when it had. And when it came to steps two and three, the ability to persuade this boy to open up could turn out to be as important as the lab work. And if it came down to getting a kid to trust her, the CDC had probably bet on the wrong horse in terms of who they had paired with Danice.

BECAUSE HELP IS WHERE YOU FIND IT

Which is where she came up with the idea of somehow getting Branislav involved. Aleq was being transferred to the BSL-4 lab at Rocky Mountain Laboratories, and she'd been informed she was going with him, since both she and Danice had vouched for the fact that she was the only one able to get anywhere at all with him in terms of eliciting information. Her first reaction to the thought of roping Branislav in had been an impatient *Really? This* is what you're concerning yourself with, at *this* point? But she also remembered the way he listened to kids, his own and those he worked with—like he wanted to absorb absolutely everything of any importance whatsoever—and the way they responded. And the way he'd helped her learn, in terms of Mirko, when to share emotional information and when to keep quiet. She mentioned the idea to Danice, who just looked at her in response. Maybe she *was* just indulging in some motivated reasoning, she admitted. And then when Danice still didn't respond, Jeannine added, "But maybe help is where you find it."

FIRE DRILL, TOWER OF BABEL

Aleq was being transferred as a partial result of a cyclonic cluster-fuck of bureaucratic hysteria and infighting of which Jeannine was only partly aware. It involved, besides the CDC's Special Pathogens Branch, Homeland Security and the DOD and some outreach feelers from USAMRIID, as well DARPA's Prophecy program, the WHO's Global Outbreak Alert and Response Network, and USAID's Emerging Pandemic Threats program. Even Google's Global Viral Forecasting Initiative had gotten involved. Whether Aleq was the index patient or Typhoid Mary or both, entities that usually agreed on almost nothing else had agreed on the critical usefulness of bringing everything available to bear on his examination. If he was a convalescent and had been infected, his blood might be the starting point for a treatment; if he was still giving off the pathogen, all of that testing would need to happen in a Level 4 environment.

And Olsen was frighteningly compelling evidence that the kid was still shedding the pathogen. If they were right about the incubation period, his initial symptoms lined up with the kid's having kicked Olsen's mask off after Olsen had tackled him. Though he could have been infected any number of other ways as well.

All of those agencies were now fully in the mix because the pathogen was breaking worldwide. They'd seen that coming, of course, and during Jeannine's first call-in the night she'd arrived in Ilulissat, when her supervisor had answered back in Atlanta, she'd said, instead of hello, "Look, we've got something here." Her supervisor would have figured that out in less than a week, anyway, when the EIS officer in special pathogens got the call from an infectious disease attending physician at a hospital in Rochester, New York, reporting three fatal cases of a weird pneumonia, after which some checking around at other hospitals across the country revealed eight additional deaths from the same thing. Given when the first reports of Ilimanaq had arrived at the CDC, they couldn't be more than eighteen or twenty days out, and so many more cases had since been flagged that the Public Affairs Division was fielding two thousand calls an hour around the clock. The staffers were getting calls at home. A triage system had had to be set up for the people working the phones, and continually recalibrated to sift out the more productive leads. And all divisions were doing what they could to deal with what Jeannine's supervisor called the inevitable second epidemic: panic.

Rumors of what had happened at Ilimanaq had generated a lot of online hysteria, but the Danish government's enforcement of the no-fly zone over the settlement had helped keep most of the postings speculative.

Improving containment had to be the key. The number of cases was growing so rapidly the containment teams were unable to keep up, and even the minimum requirement of basic record keeping was becoming untenable. Medical staffs were already so worn out and terrified they were making more and more mistakes when not feeling like everything was futile. Right then everyone's number one and two priorities needed to be how to keep the infected alive and how to break the chain of person-to-person transmission.

In Greenland, the Ministry of Health, at the direction of the prime minister, had announced the formation of mobile medical units to carry out close inspections of the infected areas and help with the quarantines, but the disease had already seeded itself around the globe. A Canadian family had had to rush their matriarch to a Berlin emergency room and then four more members of the family to a Toronto emergency room upon their return home, and the chains of infection had spiraled outward from there. Five American women who'd commandeered the Canadians' table at the airport's food court had flown from there to Rome and Palermo and then back home to New York, Charlotte, and Baltimore. A surgeon sick on his Paris-to-Hanoi flight had walked up and down the aisles of his 350-seat Airbus A350 in misery before finally being stretchered off upon landing. He'd been taken to the French Hospital, but by the time his family had had him medevaced to Hong Kong, two and then four and then nine more cases had been recorded, and five days after that half the hospital's staff had been infected and the WHO officer who'd been called in had herded all the healthy into the cafeteria and directed them to wear every piece of protective gear the hospital had in stock. When that hadn't worked, he had had the building's central air switched off, and two days after that, there had only been enough healthy staff remaining to care for the hospital's own sick personnel, so it had shut its doors.

A seventy-eight-year-old writer had carried the pathogen into Madrid, where it had killed her and then her two sons a week later, and had spread through the hospital where they'd died, infecting forty-four other patients and staff, twenty-eight of whom had died. One of the infected was a Panamanian nursing attendant who had flown home and, though she'd been feeling under the weather, had done some holiday shopping and visiting and thereby had started additional chains of infection there. A Lithuanian sick in Vilnius had stopped by an emergency room before hopping on a train to his home city of Kaunas, where he'd infected another hospital before being transferred to a third. A Peruvian visiting Lisbon had thrown up in the lobby and the fifteenth-floor corridor of his hotel, infecting an international conference of ophthalmologists, and an old friend who'd visited him in the hospital had ended up back in the same hospital herself, as had her husband and daughters and sister, and within two weeks there had been enough health care workers incapacitated from the same pathogen to overfill two entire wards.

No one in the medical community had had to mention that this thing's potential for transmission when it came to caregivers and medical personnel was extraordinary. The week after the WHO had issued its global alert, its chief of the Northern European office had reported that two of his own staff members were infected.

Jeannine's supervisor told her on one of their calls that his best friend, the chief of internal medicine at Sibley Memorial, had developed a fever and a cough and had put herself in isolation and had her family quarantine themselves in their home, but had also celebrated her twenty-fifth wedding anniversary the night before, and so all of those guests now needed to be tracked down. And when Jeannine had answered, "Well, weren't *you* at that party?" her supervisor had told her that yes, he had been. And then they'd both gone quiet on the line, before he'd broken the silence by telling her that as someone who had now seen more cases of this than anyone, she could qualify as the world's foremost expert on the subject.

When she got off the phone she thought about the way her basic relations had changed, as they had with COVID-19. People approaching, people near her space: she registered it now with a trace of hostility, like a justified misanthrope.

For every person who got sick, how many others were they going to infect? They had a pretty good idea of the incubation period, but they didn't know how long the infected were contagious or the size of the susceptible population. The best estimates were that there were already some 71,000 cases in eighteen countries by this point—roughly week three—and that if the current rates of infection held up they were headed very quickly for 280,000 by week five, and from there the outlook got worse.

If Ilimanaq was any indication, the susceptible population was everybody, but so far the mortality rate in Ililussat hadn't been nearly as high, and no one knew why.

Most governments' websites were urging calm and listing all

of the measures being taken, including mask mandates and shut-downs and bans and the ongoing efforts to develop a test, while the global news outlets panicked at different volumes—Jeannine's recent favorite was the Fox graphic "APOCALYPSE II?"—but all of that seemed trampled by the social media cacophony, none of which practiced or urged restraint. In America the right wing alter-nated between claiming that there was no real problem and that the problem was now under control. Both positions were mocked and debunked, but the net effect was to create further paralysis, or, as Jeannine's mother complained to her in one email, "Everyone says something different."

And every morning Marie Louisa redirected their attention from what was happening worldwide to the problem at hand, when she briefed them on the hospital's latest fatalities and new cases.

Danice's mom kept phoning and pitching emails into the white-out of all of the other emails with which Danice had to deal, pleading for updates and advice, and Danice told Jeannine that she'd wanted to tell her mother that the short answer was "How would I know?" But instead she forwarded the standard recommended precautions that everyone remembered from COVID-19: wear a mask, practice social distancing, avoid touching your face, wash your hands with soap and water, sanitize surfaces, avoid sharing utensils and food, and so on. Her mom emailed back, "Thanks so much," and added an emoji with an exasperated expression.

Jeannine's supervisor, after a long, dispirited phone call one late night, had suggested that maybe it was time for some humility when it came to acknowledging that science had come up empty-handed so far. And that maybe they had to concede that there were all sorts of phenomena they were unable to not only understand but in some cases even identify. And that maybe it would help to remember that this was how medical science and scientific knowledge evolved, any-way. When Jeannine had agreed with all of that, he'd added that they were just going to have to hope for something really rare in the history of microbiology: that all of the knowledge the scientific community was currently lacking developed *very* quickly.

What happened next was probably going to depend not so much on the science as the politics. As everyone had recently been reminded, usually when medicine collided with culture, medicine lost, and while some governments rapidly facilitated containment efforts, others just made things worse. China had already locked down some five cities and forty million people and was establishing dragnets and requiring neighbors to inform on one another, while in the U.S. the spokesperson for America's Health Insurance Plans, the industry's lobbying group, had announced that the industry would be *not* be waiving copayments for any treatments. In the four military bases in Texas, California, Montana, and North Carolina that had been prepared to house the infected, the uninsured would receive free housing and board, but no medications, though individuals could rotate out as they passed the incubation period.

Russia, India, North Korea, and the UK had ordered the expulsion of any and all foreigners with symptoms. All over the world, health care systems were being besieged by the panicking healthy while great numbers of the infected refused hospitalization no matter how sick they got. Outbreaks that created chaos in rural areas created bedlam in urban ones.

Qatar and Kuwait had banned flights to and from Iceland and Denmark and Germany until further notice. The United Arab Emirates now sprayed pesticides in all aircraft arriving from infected countries. In Germany, medical teams were boarding all incoming flights to check for illness before anyone was allowed to disembark. Border checkpoints were closing to infected countries. And most hospitals had had to resort to armed guards provided by the military to enforce their quarantines.

THE SECOND EPIDEMIC

Olsen crashed the next morning and his daughter that afternoon and they couldn't save either of them. Danice had been helping out and showed Jeannine the marks on her wrist where he had grabbed her. She said his daughter had heard him calling for her before he died. Marie Louisa was beside herself with grief and had developed her own symptoms, and with her even temporarily out of commission the wheels started to come off the system she'd helped set up. Her assistant head nurse seemed to be continually making tea in a state of paralyzed panic, and the doctor now in charge—one of those who had been laid low when Jeannine and Danice had arrived, maybe by something totally unrelated, and had since recovered—seemed to regard them as though they had brought the bug to Greenland themselves. Volunteers who'd been making home visits and following up contacts looking for signs of illness were refusing to keep working. Three of the cleaning staff had barricaded themselves in an apartment with some food supplies. A cruise ship had arrived in the harbor, and Jeannine had had to argue with the captain that dropping anchor wasn't such a good idea. And then, in the understatement of the week, Danice had remarked that morale seemed to have been further eroded by the announcement that the prime minister had been flown to Denmark to better direct the emergency measures.

Jeannine's supervisor told her in exasperation how much of his time was being gobbled up in fielding urgent demands from USAM-RIID and Homeland Security and the DARPA program—whose motto was "Creating and Preventing Strategic Surprise"—on the subject of whether it was possible that they were dealing here with a weaponized pathogen. Everyone mostly agreed that given what looked to be the probable point of origin—if Ground Zero *was* Ilimanaq—it seemed unlikely that something had walked out of a lab. Or had been released, her supervisor agreed. He added that he'd told all of the bio-warriors who'd been busting his stones that they probably didn't need to go looking for Dr. No on this one, since as they already knew from COVID-19, nature itself was weaponizing pathogens all the time.

He also told Jeannine to saddle up and get ready to leave on the National Guard C-130 that was coming for the boy from Ilimanaq. Its ETA right now was 0600 the next morning and there'd be an Air Transport Isolation System in the cargo bay and techies to run it, along with some nurses, an MD, and an infectious disease guy. Because whatever this was was still unknown, she should destroy the ISO-POD she'd used to get Aleq to Ilulissat, just to be safe.

She asked who'd be coming to replace her and he told her it would be Jerry Sussman, the guy who spoke Danish and who'd had the flu when the first call had come in.

"He's got a lot of years in," the supervisor told her. "He'll do fine."

"Has Danice ever worked with him before?" Jeannine wanted to know.

"I have no idea," her supervisor said.

"How's *your* health, by the way?" she asked.

"Knock on wood," he told her. "Though apparently three people from that party have already come down with something."

SORRY TO LEAVE YOU WITH ALL THIS

Somewhere over the Atlantic she got a text from Danice that Olsen's wife had died. *The whole family*, Jeannine thought. Recognitions like that jolted her in this new state she was in, and then she moved on. Danice added that Marie Louisa was still hanging in there.

Saying their goodbyes, Jeannine and Danice had been dry-eyed going through everything they had to go over, but once they'd finished, Danice had asked her if she'd had a lot of good friends over the years, and they'd both lost it. While they were wiping their eyes, Danice told her that during her entire childhood her mother had never once admitted to being sad. And that even when Danice had caught her mother weeping, sitting by herself in the laundry room, her mother had admitted only to having had "the mopes."

Jeannine gave her a smile, and asked, "You going to be okay here?"

Danice closed her eyes like she was giving it some real thought, and said, "The other thing my mother always says to anyone who'll listen is, 'And *I'm* going to have to be the one to *clean up* this mess.'" She gave Jeannine a grim smile. "She'll probably tell me I had this coming."

"My mother's version of that is always 'Oh, honey, *you* can handle *this*,'" Jeannine told her. "And then she always gives me this look, like she loves me but I have *no idea* what's about to hit me."

They stayed facing each other until someone finally rapped at the door and said in English that some people were waiting for Dr. Dziri.

"I love you," Danice told her. "I'm scared about being here without you."

"I love you too," Jeannine answered. "You'll be fine."

At first Danice told her she was too busy to come out to the airport, but then she did anyway, and she waved and watched Jeannine climb aboard the Hercules, and then turned away before the rear cargo ramp had fully shut.

WELCOME TO BSL-4

Rocky Mountain Laboratories turned out to be in Hamilton, Montana, surrounded by a high black metal fence in a residential neighborhood with one- or two-story homes all around it, with the mountains rising beyond them just out of town. Soon after 9/11, the president and Congress had authorized the National Institute of Allergy and Infectious Diseases to increase its research into effective biowarfare countermeasures and had ponied up $66 million for an enhanced biosafety lab—a BSL-4—and the RML had been chosen because first, it had had the basic infrastructure already in place, and second, the location was sufficiently remote if something went kablooey. The new lab was called the Integrated Research Facility, had opened in 2008, and was all about shared spaces and resources, the idea being to get everyone from scientists to administrators to animal care staff talking to one another as much as possible. Jeannine had gotten more of the lab's history from the chief of virology after the ride in from the airfield, during the security procedures, which were beyond comprehensive. At the front gate, you went through a security cottage manned by an armed guard and then a metal detector, and everything you were carrying was sent through an imager, while you showed your clearance and signed in and received your ID. Entry to each lab following that involved another ID, with the BSL-4 in its own separate building and requiring yet more security, with more armed guards and metal detectors and all the rest of it, as well as an iris scan, which, Jeannine was informed, wouldn't work if someone propped a corpse in front of the lens. "Well, I guess there's no point in dragging around dead Uncle Charlie, then," she remarked, but the guy working the scan didn't laugh.

She was asked a lot about Aleq and recounted much of what she knew. The chief asked her to call him Hank and wanted to know how Aleq had held up on the long flight. She said the big issue for him had been the burial of his loved ones, and that she was yet to deliver on her promise to show him pictures of their graves. Hank looked at her like he was waiting for more, so she added that the Danes had sent a military unit in hazmat suits to Ilimanaq, and that she was waiting for some Danish pilots who had promised to send photos once they had them. He asked if she thought the little settlement had been Ground Zero, and she said that if she had to say right now, she'd say yes. He nodded, and told her they'd come up with a Danish speaker who'd be listening in and translating into her earpiece—had she ever worn this kind of earpiece?—though the Wi-Fi was spotty with these new ones for some reason. She tried it on and asked when she'd be getting started and he answered as soon as she was ready.

YOU AND ME AND ZERO ROOM FOR ERROR

She had logged a fair number of hours in BSL-4 labs before, and only needed to be brought up to speed on a few new features in the clothing room while she and Emily, the director of the Division of Microbiology and Infectious Diseases, changed into disposable underwear and surgical scrubs, since no personal clothing was allowed in. Normally the director wouldn't be scrubbing in on something like this, she told Jeannine, but since nearly everyone in the building wanted in on this—the heads of bacteriology and mycology, respiratory diseases, and virology, especially, just to name three—she thought this might help her figure out how best to divvy up the access.

"Even if we try to keep it to a minimum, there's going to be a lot of coming and going around your boy," Emily told her. "We're going to be relying on you to provide him some continuity and reassurance."

"Well, I think he'd be surprised to hear he's *my* boy," Jeannine told her. "I'm hardly his dream come true. But I'm the best he's got, I guess."

It turned out he'd freaked out at having been separated from her on the drive in from the airfield, and had had to be sedated again.

"He's gone through a lot," Jeannine explained, after a minute, once she'd been told.

"I can only imagine," Emily agreed.

"Jewelry?" she asked before they passed into the second room with the suits, and Jeannine shook her head. The suits were spread out for inspection, and they plugged in the air hoses suspended in coils from the ceiling, listened for the waterfall sounds of the airflow, and inflated their suits empty for integrity testing, squeezing and checking in particular those areas that wore out the fastest: the gloves, the seams around the visor, and the feet. Fully inflated, the suits looked a little comical, like astronauts' versions of sex dolls. After the visual inspection they put their ears to the various seams, and then deflated the suits and stepped into them feet first, slid them over their arms, and stretched and worked their fingers into the outer gloves. Then they pulled the clear bonnets over their heads and hooked up the air and closed their front zippers. They braced each other while they pulled on big outer boots that looked like children's rain boots. Then they unhooked, hung up their hoses, and passed through the airlock. The inner door only released its gaskets if the door that had just been passed through was sealed. Then they hooked up again inside the lab. The same procedure would operate in reverse on the way out, except they'd also get a chemical shower.

Jeannine got around okay, though she always forgot how even sitting down with the hose and tether was a minor adventure. She dropped a pipette while she was getting a sample tray ready at a workstation, but otherwise everything went smoothly, though she saw Emily raise an eyebrow in her own suit, as if to remind the newbie that 99 out of 100 wouldn't cut it here.

Besides their new earpieces there was a cell phone that always stayed in the facility, since the rule was that anyone at work in the lab always had to have someone outside the lab but in the building with whom they had an open line of communication. God knew how anyone was supposed to hear anything on the cell phone through the blowing air in the suits.

A lot of the BSL-4 labs didn't have the facilities to handle patients, but the RML had three rooms for that, and a mini ICU.

They'd be coming at Aleq from as many angles as they could think of, but the two main ones were going to be scouring him for some trace of the pathogen—they had the antibodies' footprints all over his samples, but maybe they could find *some* hint of the shoe that had made them?—and extracting more information from his memory. There was, it turned out, another line of infection that had broken out in Nuuk, and from there had traveled to Copenhagen and possibly beyond. It seemed to be presenting somewhat different symptoms and, more important, so far hadn't seemed to have had any connection to Ilimanaq. Was this an entirely different pathogen, or a possible mutation? Danice and everyone back in Atlanta were hoping that someone out of the initial group infected in Nuuk *had* in fact come from or passed through Ilimanaq, and so thirty-three photos of those dead and alive that had been the first ones sick in Nuuk had been forwarded to the lab so Jeannine could walk the boy through them.

But their reunion in the room they'd set up for him was such a disaster that ten minutes into it she could see Emily's dismay even through her attempted poker face. The nurse technician kept miming for Aleq how to hook on the earpiece and microphone and he kept tossing it onto the bed next to him. She repeatedly retrieved it and pointed to Jeannine, doing her best to suggest that the former would enable communication with the latter, but the boy responded as though she were pointing to the wall. Jeannine gave it a try, gesturing to her ear and then to him, but only produced a change in his expression when she and the nurse technician had had to untangle their air hoses. And he wouldn't even look at the Nuuk patients' photos on her iPad. She'd found herself angling it around in front of his averted face until she'd finally given up.

"He's probably still feeling a lot of the sedation," Emily told her.

He gave them no trouble when the nurse technician collected some lung and blood cells, even as invasive as the first procedure was.

"He probably just needs a little more time to get used to all of this," Emily added once they were out of the unit and stripping down for the chemical shower. She didn't sound very convinced.

"You should see what he's like with people he *doesn't* trust," Jeannine joked, but Emily just looked at her in response.

SEEMS LIKE OLD TIMES

He still had his old cell number and she FaceTimed him and he picked up on the third ring. He had a thicker beard and was wearing a white V-neck T-shirt and seemed to be in a room with nothing whatsoever on the walls. "Look who's calling," he said. The lack of warmth in his voice pierced her, and she registered that he was still the guy who'd been left in charge of either expanding or tightening her chest.

"How've you been?" she asked.

"Everybody's healthy here," he said. "I assume you're in the middle of all of this?"

She'd set up an Instagram account a while ago but never posted anything on it and didn't know why she would have expected him to have checked it, anyway.

"Oh yeah," she said.

"And is it as bad as some people say it is?" he asked.

"Oh yeah," she said.

"So how can I help you?" he said.

"Well, it's nice to see you, too," she joked.

"Jeannine," he said. He rubbed his eyes with his free hand. From what she could see he was slumped across one chair and had his legs up over another. He looked directly at the camera and adjusted his expression. She was sure how hard this was was written all over her face, but he had perfected this look which indicated an unwillingness to notice stuff he found inconvenient. It was the expression she remembered from after Mirko's death, when he would come home from work and catch her eye and they would go about their routines.

They had just mutually pulled onto this road of not being together. In the face of her guilt and misery he had gotten more and more passive in his disappointment, like he'd been watching someone else's kid's bad behavior. And when he got like that, she had imagined that she'd been being circumspect in her responses, but had only figured out afterward that she'd really just been cold. She remembered once after they'd had sex looking from her bed at one of his shirts in her closet and startling herself with the way it seemed like evidence of their future breakup.

"Jeannine?" he asked.

She told him she needed his help with Aleq. She gave him a rundown of the situation, trying to remember everything that was crucial, and he listened and didn't say anything for a long time until she finally felt like she'd run out of sentences.

"And I can just walk into a place like that?" he asked.

"You won't be in the hot lab," she said. "You may be interfacing with him on a screen. Or through a headset. Or maybe just advising me."

"They don't have their own people for something like that?" he wanted to know. "Some kind of call list?"

"I argued for you," she told him. "And I reminded them that whoever that person is, he has to work well with me."

He seemed to be thinking about what she had said and was looking down and away from the camera. The first time she had kissed him, he had just come out of her bathroom and she had been waiting in the hallway. She'd backed him up and braced herself against the wall with both hands. When she pulled out memories like that for herself, she sometimes wondered if she was accessing the same remnant or just throwing together a whole new assembly to accommodate her needs. Once he'd left her, their past had become this ongoing saga for her, and if she'd had more friends, it probably would've become part of an oral tradition.

At one point when she'd maxed out her self-pity during their breakup he had reminded her of a little speech she'd given him after lovemaking only a few weeks into their relationship. While his hands had still been stroking her hips, she'd provided her theory of Relationship Phases, with phase 1 being that first buzz of interest, phase 2 that initial excitement at how much you had in common, phase 3 the exhilaration at your capacity for merger, phase 4 those aspects of the gift you started to take for granted, phase 5 the initial demonstrations with other people that you *didn't* have your partner's back, and phase 6 when you started thinking, *Maybe the problem is me.*

She remembered him saying, "*That's* the theory you want to run by me right now?" and she'd tried to suggest in response that she'd just been joshing around. But it had changed the temperature between them. For that reason she had brought it up again a few weeks later, and he hadn't seemed to want to talk about it.

"So this kid has clearly latched on to you, for all of his wariness, and you don't feel like you can help him," Branislav said, and she found herself unable to answer. She remembered finding Mirko in the kitchen one night trying to make a sandwich in the dark. When she'd asked why he hadn't turned on the light, he'd said, "You hate when I turn on lights."

"I need your help," she repeated. "*He* needs your help."

Branislav looked into the camera again for a while, like once more she had disappointed him in ways he couldn't have predicted.

"What am I gonna do?" he finally said. "Refuse to try to save the world?"

She had no idea what was going on on her face, but he wasn't looking at it anyhow. "Thank you," she told him.

He said, "Just let me know how soon they'll be here."

VI

✢ ✢ ✢ ✢ ✢ ✢ ✢ ✢ ✢ ✢ ✢ ✢ ✢ ✢ ✢ ✢ ✢ ✢ ✢ ✢

IV

Most of the first half of the staff meeting had been devoted to how the quarantine was going, and the bottom line had been that it didn't appear as though their hospital had had the best performance in the region, though it didn't look like they had had the worst, either. Some hospitals were already in desperate shape. There were some memes from Community Memorial in Hamilton that were tagged "Land of the Lost."

Val's intern from Oklahoma, Ronnie, had been one of the first to get sick, followed by four of the nurses and nine members of the first three boys' families, and since then, three staff members and two more of the attendings had been infected, and the infectious disease guy was telling everyone that he didn't feel good, either. Some of the patients had hung on, while the nurse who had performed the initial intubations on Aaron and Kenny had been on a respirator by the middle of the day after her first symptoms and then had been dead before dark.

Val had liked her, and had teased her about being one of those new moms who the week after she brought her baby home had reconsidered her whole apartment for hazards and had replaced her glass coffee table with an ottoman.

Sometimes this thing killed very quickly and sometimes it didn't. It was unnerving that they hadn't made more progress on why, other than the extra vulnerability created by some obvious preconditions.

The intensive care unit had, fortunately, recently been updated with a control room and video banks that not only monitored all the rooms but also provided vital signs to let the staff know round the clock who was short of breath, who was hypoxemic, and who was just rolling over, and it had been expanded and given responsibility for all suspected cases. After the first nurse had died, the unit had been closed to patients with any other conditions, and they'd managed to scrounge up enough masks with particulate filters, and the interview room had been converted to a dressing area for those about to enter the unit. There'd been some talk of a guard for the door, but it had turned out that no one who didn't have to went anywhere near it, anyway, and everyone inside was by this point too sick to try to get out.

The second half of the meeting was supposed to be dedicated to brainstorming solutions for the optimal ways of proceeding, but everyone was constantly distracted with calls from other hospitals and doctors and panicked relatives and other alarming posts and news bits and rumors on their phones. And it was hard not to keep coming back to the mystery of what they were dealing with, and the possibility that it was something they were just failing to recognize and they were all going to look stupid when the obvious explanation turned up. The calls were coming in partially because when they had first started talking about this as a group, the unanimous conclusion had been to throw the problem open to every conceivable medical expert, and now every idea that had occurred to anyone who'd been contacted was pouring in. Val understood the impulse and had fired off a few theories herself to some of her old teachers, since anything felt more proactive than just sitting around baffled and frightened.

When she had first called around to her friends at other hospitals, they hadn't seen a single case, but now they were all trying to figure out where to get more resources for the number they were dealing with.

In the meantime, they were still following the protocols and charting everything they could, including demographic information, the patterns of the presentations, the pulmonary and cardiac findings, and the responses to the various treatments.

In more normal situations they would have been instructed to stop working on the infected material immediately and to transfer all remaining specimens to the CDC. But this seemed to be already almost everywhere, and so Val imagined that the CDC's ability to follow up on noncompliance had evaporated. But it was hard to know what was going on anywhere with any certainty.

And, of course, to make everything worse, the media was in full-on the-sky-is-falling mode 24/7, and that shaded over into scapegoat mode—what had the CDC known, and when had it known it? And *had* this bug been smuggled into the West by undocumented aliens?—and while Fox News had outdone itself this time around when it came to its public irresponsibility (*Were* the Democrats trying to mandate that the infected homeless be brought into otherwise safe health centers?), even despite all of that, ten minutes on social media made you nostalgic for the relative restraint of what was left of the mainstream. Checking your Twitter feed took more courage than base jumping, and everyone knew someone who could show them videos so terrifying that the most ubiquitous hashtag had now become something you said to people when they waved these images in front of you: "GTSAM," pronounced *Get-Sam*, for "Get That Shit Away from Me." Whenever you got a moment to yourself you picked up your phone and panicked again.

A big thunderstorm knocked out the power for a few minutes and everyone in the meeting had to shut the open windows against the rain. Not necessarily what you wanted in a building filled with airborne pathogens.

"What's the most serious outbreak of anything the world's ever seen?" Val's other intern, Sally, asked out of the darkness, while they all sat there listening to the wind and rain on the glass.

"Human beings," the chief attending said. There were some *You got* that *right* chuckles.

"And *all* outbreaks eventually come to an end," another attending noted. The infectious disease guy was missing, having just gone into quarantine. There was a little box of Kleenex where he usually sat. No one was sitting near it.

The chief attending looked around the table. "Remember when *one* resident getting sick would throw everything into chaos?" he reminisced.

On a break in the cafeteria she sorted through her mother's most recent complaints. Three grim nurses were at the table beside her, leaning forward over their plastic cups. They were scrolling through their phones and outdoing each other with upsetting stuff they found. Beyond them a staff member was washing the floor.

Her mother had sent a video of Val's sister sitting by herself in the living room, weeping. Val wasn't sure how it was supposed to operate as an accusation, but she texted back, *How about next time giving her a hug instead of filming her?* After a minute her mother answered, *This was after the hug.*

Even on good days Val had never found it easy to reconcile her workload with what were supposed to be her obligations as a family member, and her mother's and sister's responses to her quarantine had been to demand hourly updates by text, and then to text her even more when ignored. Her sister often added in links to stories from CNN or the *Daily Mail* with headlines like "DOOMSDAY IN THE U.K." The previous Christmas Eve, Val's mother had sat her down and walked her through all of the various ways in which Val had failed her sister, who had a good job at a PR firm but also periodically got blackout drunk and had found herself one morning a few months before that on the maintenance platform of a highway billboard in a driving rain.

Lori looked up to her, her mother had reminded her, and just because she hadn't been very receptive didn't mean that Val couldn't be more persistent. Val had responded that it reminded her of that old question of who was more neglected by the doctor's lifestyle, the doctor or her family, and her mother had said, "Well, in *this* case, the family."

Kirk, at least, had eased off on the *What's going on?* texts, and his attitude toward panic was that it was mostly for cucks, a word he loved and Val deplored, and that medicine was all about having to do something before you were really ready to do it, and that you just needed to remind yourself that whatever it was you were trying to do could definitely be done.

She had always had more patience with guys who were self-sufficient, which was how she'd stayed with him for two years. She'd met him on a surgery rotation but they hadn't gotten together until a few years after that, and she told friends who hadn't met him yet that he was that guy who had the button on his white rounds coat that read "The Way to Heal Is With Cold Steel." He was usually even busier than she was. He had also turned out to be, among other things, a spontaneous spelunker, which she'd only discovered on a walk when he had spotted a grassy gap under an overhanging rock and had disappeared into it for so long she'd ended up deciding to meet him later at a nearby coffee shop. He'd texted her, *Already 30 ft down! Come on in!* and she'd texted back directions to the coffee shop.

He also considered himself very handy with tools and had built some simple end tables for her and seemed to think that that made them very close. But that was the guy he every so often wanted to be, not the guy he was. And she was the same way. She reminded herself of this blind woman she'd met in med school—and how *that* had worked had never failed to amaze her—who *every day* had had this incredibly patient guy appear to pick her up after class to take her where she needed to go, a guy who was clearly over the moon about her. Another class member had said to the blind woman in front of the guy, "That is *so* sweet," and the guy had opened his mouth to respond and the blind woman had answered, "We're not really a thing."

Almost the entire Friedman family—Aaron, his mother, father, grandfather, and older brother Andrew—had been wiped out; the youngest brother, Abraham, was still hanging on. He was nine. He had no visitors. No one to talk with him or read with him or watch TV with him or hold his hand during the most difficult procedures. One of the saddest aspects of his situation was how quietly he handled the unfairness of it all. It was like whatever was coming, he'd already figured out he was going to be dealing with it alone. He was always on a laptop Val had lent him looking up stuff about the outbreak.

He was having more trouble breathing and his blood oxygen numbers were getting worse and worse, and when he asked her about it she didn't lie to him, but she also told him that things might turn around and he might start finding it easier to breathe soon. His numbers were heading in the wrong direction, but some things you kept to yourself. Patients didn't need to hear everything.

Instead she gave him a smile, though he was smart enough to interpret it. He was watching videos on YouTube of someone exploding groundhogs with rifle fire, and the way he looked at her before he returned his attention to the screen reminded her that she'd probably become the only focus he could find for all of the feelings he had left.

He asked her not to leave him, so she sat with him for a little while, but her beeper kept going off and she had things to do, so she told him she'd be back soon, and then collapsed for five minutes in the break room. There were six other people in there with her, three of them sound asleep, and everybody had masks on and little hand sanitizer bottles hooked to their belts.

It was sunny outside, and there was a nice breeze coming in the open windows. Every morning it looked like the garbage in the streets had increased overnight. If all of this hadn't happened, most colleges would've been starting their spring break soon.

Another text arrived from her sister, and she just stared at it. It was like the other part of her life had broken off in a landslide.

She spent an hour with two other patients who were holding steady, and when Abraham crashed she was only the fourth or fifth person to get to the room. When she arrived the chief attending was looking at his watch and counting the pulse even though those numbers were up on one of the monitors, and someone called that the kid wasn't breathing and the chief attending shouted for everyone to get organized and out of each other's way. Val was standing behind him and when he was finished with his compressions she did hers and then moved to the back of the line of others waiting to take their turn. She did one more set and was in the middle of the line for the next one when they gave up on Abraham and called it, and, after another traumatic minute or two, they turned off the monitors.

She had barely known the boy, with his little brown bangs and big ears. His chest looked a little sunken and his arms a little higher from all of the compressions, and he was still looking upward like he'd been stunned by the ceiling tiles. Val couldn't look at him and couldn't look away. She wasn't sure how long it was before someone led her out into the hall and sat her in the break room with a Styrofoam cup of water in her hand.

When things had quieted a little, afterward, someone came to get her to attend the meeting for the team that had managed the code to review what might have been done better. She didn't catch a lot of what was said, but when someone asked her some direct questions, she put in her two cents and then sat there thinking that just a few hours ago the boy had been served his lunch and had wanted her to bring him her laptop and had teased her about her password. She thought about his brother Aaron: if he'd just not gone on that trip. If he'd just turned left instead of right, gone up instead of down, done whatever instead of whatever. Her mentor in med school had reminded her more than once that doctors got even less time than families had to deal with patients dying. Someone died and the relatives went off by themselves and collapsed, but you still had the rest of your shift to get through.

At least she didn't have to transition to small talk with her mother and sister.

Why had this boy's death rocked her more than some of the others she'd just been through? She didn't know.

The chief attending was a nice guy and sat with her for a little while. "You want some tea?" he asked. She shook her head, and he nodded like he already knew that. He reminded her that every lousy outcome was ten times more powerful than a save. He said that when it came to what was doing the killing, it seemed pretty clear that multiple causes were converging in a cascade. She agreed. He waited, and then made a big exhausted noise himself, and told her to take care. After he left, she got herself up and into a bathroom.

In the mirror she had that shot-out-of-a-cannon look she remembered from an intern who hadn't worked out, who'd been so inept they'd called him Double O, as in licensed to kill. The first time one of his admissions had died, he'd been so shell-shocked he'd sat down for lunch with nothing on his tray but silverware, and had not seemed to notice that there was a conversation going on around him.

She cracked her knee on the doorframe leaving the bathroom, but she was so tired everything felt like it was happening somewhere else. She vaguely remembered during her initial anatomy exam in med school wandering from station to station, each station featuring a body part she'd definitely never seen before, and the way she'd started to feel as though she were being pranked.

At some point the news that the disease seemed to be everywhere around them broke down the logic of the quarantine. Early on everyone had looked to the CDC for guidelines and the CDC had sent out PDFs and videos of quarantine procedures and lengths, but all of these had seemed to envision scenarios in which the outbreak was relatively contained. Pressure had grown from the staff to be allowed to visit loved ones, and then the head nurse's mom had gotten sick and she'd been so distraught that the chief attending had let her go home for a day, and she'd come back a little restored and still healthy, and so after that a few more favored staff members who seemed have remained healthy, once they were checked out as fully as they could be for traces of the disease, were allowed to go home after long stretches on call, with various precautions, for twenty-four hours at a time.

When the chief attending came back into the room to check on Val, she said, "Maybe *I* should take a break. You know: if we're still letting people out."

"You do look like you could use one," he said.

She gave him what she imagined was a wan smile. "One of my mother's texts the other day said, *They can't keep you there forever. Can they?*"

"Any sniffles? Respiratory issues?" he asked.

She did a bodybuilder's arm curl and flexed her bicep.

"Well, we *can't* keep everybody here forever," he conceded.

A nurse cracked open the door and peeked in like she didn't want to disturb anyone. "Ronnie's struggling again," she told Val.

The chief attending followed them to the room Ronnie was in. "Where in Oklahoma is he from?" he asked before they got there.

"Tulsa," Val told him. Right after she got to the room, two nurses wheeled a crash cart in behind her, and Ronnie said in a way that pierced her, "Hi, Dr. Landry."

"How're we doing, Ronnie?" she asked.

"I woulda said okay until a minute ago," he told her.

"You gonna let a little bug worry you?" she asked him.

He gave her a small smile and closed his eyes and shook his head.

She upped the oxygen to 28 percent on his venturi mask, and that seemed to settle him down, though his face stayed flushed and his tremors shook the mattress. After a short wait his oxygen levels were up again, so everyone relaxed a little. He looked like he'd conked out, and she smoothed his hair and went back out into the corridor with the chief attending.

"So what do you think, about that break?" she asked him. He stretched his arm out down the hallway in response, like a doorman pointing the way across a lobby.

VINEGAR

When she called her mother to tell her she was coming home, her mother burst out crying and said that she'd see her soon, and then called back and asked if it was really safe for her to be coming home, and then called back again after that and reminded her that Lori always got sick easier than she did, and said that she just wanted to make sure that Val was doing the right thing.

"So does your boss think that you can't spread it?" she asked, after Val had made no response.

"Nobody knows anything, Ma," Val said. "This is our best guess. I've been working on the ward for quite a bit longer than what we think is the incubation period for the thing, and I haven't been near any of the new arrivals, and I feel good, other than being tired. And they checked me out as best they could. Do you want me to *not* come home?"

"Come home, come home," her mother told her.

"Can we hug?" her mother asked at the front door. Her mask had a pattern of strawberries on it. Val said they didn't need to take extra chances, so her mother waited until Val had gotten her coat off and changed into sweatpants and flopped down onto their sofa before asking her if they were any closer to figuring out what this thing was. When Val said that as far as she knew, no one had any idea, her mother wanted to know if Val had asked her boss. Her mother was like some of the older patients on Val's rounds who tended to be very sweet to her before they asked when they were going to get to see the doctor.

While her mother set the table she explained to Val that her neighbor was convinced it was the coronavirus and that the government just wasn't telling people, and that they'd be splitting eight manicotti because that's what she'd been able to dig out of the freezer. She and Lori had gone to both Herrema's and the Price Rite and both had been cleaned out.

"There was *nothing* on the shelves?" Val wanted to know.

"Like, vinegar," Lori called from upstairs. "Hot sauce."

They also had a can of beans in the cupboard, her mother added. And the Price Rite guy had told her that as far as he knew, the regular Monday deliveries would still be happening.

She opened the beans and dumped them into a little pot with some water. "You have about twenty minutes," she said. By which Val understood her to mean *Go up and say hello to your sister.*

She heaved herself off the sofa, but when she passed her mother, her mother held the back of her hand up toward Val's cheek. "You look tired," her mother said.

"Yep," Val said.

"You don't seem warm," her mother suggested.

"Nope," Val agreed.

"I know you're working hard, but I hope you're not overdoing it," her mother said. "You can only do what you can do."

"Sometimes you can't even do that," Val said.

"Oh, honey: I'm sure you're helping a lot of people," her mother said. She'd told Val years ago that she hadn't been sure that Val could *be* a doctor, though she *had* been sure that Val was stubborn enough to stay at it, and that Val was certainly smarter than anyone else in the house, and when push had come to shove, Val's mother and father had each taken on double shifts to help pay Val's tuition.

At the top of the stairs, Val stalled outside of Lori's room, half amused and half irritated that even now her sister was making her jump through these kinds of stupid hoops.

She pushed open the door. Lori was at her desk staring out the window. The desk was from when she was a kid, and at this point she was way too large for it, and for some reason that always moved Val.

"Did you hear that Joey Kiely died?" Lori said. She was wearing an old bandanna as her mask. She got up and came over to give Val a hug, but Val held up a hand. She was a big woman and bent a little as if to adjust herself to Val's height. Joey Kiely was a boy they'd played with as kids. "And his mom, too," Lori added.

"No," Val said, and ran a palm up and down her own sleeve.

"Ellis is shut down for the time being," Lori said. "So I've been home all week and she's been driving me nuts." Ellis was her PR firm.

"She's been enjoying quality time with her favorite daughter," Val told her.

"So has it been as awful as I would think?" Lori wanted to know.

In the corner, some board games were still stacked in a Jenga-like tower half the height of the dresser. Dirty and clean clothes were flung everywhere. Her sister's softball bat and some trophies were heaped in the open closet.

"We just lost a nine-year-old I really liked," Val told her, surprising herself. Lori looked at her with such sympathy it made Val's eyes water. "He'd already lost his whole family. He handled it better than I've handled losing my car keys."

"Sorry," Lori said.

"Thanks," Val said.

"Have you heard of anybody getting any closer to figuring out what's going on?" Lori asked. "Every so often something on the news feed gets your hopes up and then nothing happens."

"A lot about it seems simple, but apparently not simple enough," Val told her.

They stood there looking at each other, since that was as helpful as anything else. "Well, don't forget what Grandma used to say," Lori finally reminded her. "'What's always inside *impossible* is *I'm possible*.'"

"If only Grandma were alive today," Val said.

"If only Grandma had known what she was talking about," Lori added.

Their mother called from downstairs that their dinner was ready.

"You know, it's not easy for us when you don't answer," Lori told her after a minute. "We're left out here in the dark, and we know you're busy, but you can't take two minutes to answer a text?"

How *had* they gotten to the point at which she couldn't get through to either of them? Val wondered, standing there with her sister. They'd been present for each other any number of times. They knew what was involved, in terms of watching out for one another. They'd remembered birthdays, and had had bonding rituals, like watching *The Bachelor* together every Monday night. Until recently they would have sworn that the three of them could have talked about anything.

"Isn't this nice," her mother said from the doorway. "Did nobody hear me yelling that dinner was ready?"

"We heard you," Lori said. "It's just that, you know, these kind of moments are more important."

"Oh, shut up," her mother said, and led them both downstairs.

When Kirk called the next night, she told him that she probably should spend the time she had with her mother and sister, and he was fine with that and then invited himself for dinner. Her mother told her that they didn't have enough to feed him, and when Val passed that along by text, Kirk texted back that he'd be in the area anyway and that he was bringing ribs.

"Your boyfriend will be here soon, in case you want to fix yourself up," her mother told her around five that evening.

She went into the bathroom and splashed her face and pulled her hair back into a ponytail and came back out into the kitchen. Water dripped off her nose.

"Very nice," her mother said grimly.

After Kirk came in and gave everyone a wave he pulled the ribs out of a shopping bag and told Val that she looked worn out, like it was a useful observation.

"My daughter's been under a bit of a strain lately," her mother explained.

"What's *that* all been about?" he asked. There was a bottle of wine in the bag, too, and he handed it over to Lori.

Val laid out some napkins, and while Lori hunted up a corkscrew, he made a face at his phone. "It's like Twitter's blowing up every ten minutes," he said.

"Every five," she told him.

"I thought you were too busy for Twitter?" he asked.

"My sister tells me," she said.

Once they sat down to eat, her mother remarked that it *had* to be a really stressful time for Kirk, as well, wasn't it? and he shrugged and said that sure, the shit was hitting the fan everywhere, but he was still doing some of his usual workload, and he reminded her that surgeons' rounds were about as basic as rounds could get. You went down the line making sure everyone was still alive, not in too much pain, and could move their extremities. You kept it simple on the back end.

Val remembered him bragging once that one of the things that patients liked about him was his laugh, which they claimed you could hear even on the other wards.

"I'm doing what I can do, but *these* are the heroes, right here," he said to her mother, pointing at Val. When Val didn't say anything in response, he added, "So what's the good word?"

"I don't know what we're going to do at this point," she told him.

"Well, I don't know about you," he said, "but *I'm* going to eat my dinner."

BOY MEETS GIRL, REVISED

After dinner they chatted for a while with everyone in the living room, and then after Lori said she was turning in, Kirk followed Val to her room and they both sat on the bed with their backs to the headboard. Her mother peeked in and pointedly left the door ajar when she withdrew, and Val got up and shut it again just out of principle.

They were almost shoulder to shoulder and he talked for a little while about what a mess his hospital was. He was genuinely at a loss about it, and she felt bad for him. He put his palm on her lower belly and she moved it away and then apologized that her moods were all over the place. She said, "I wish I could kiss you," and he reached over and pulled their masks down and kissed her.

"That was dumb," she said.

"That was important," he told her.

He took his phone out again and was flipping through feeds with his thumb. "Don't look at that stuff," she requested. He set it down.

She put her face in her hands and said again that she didn't know what they were going to do.

He said he didn't know either. "I guess we either keep working or pack it in and grab a beer at the pity party," he told her.

"Somebody's gonna get a handle on this soon," he added, after she didn't respond.

"How're you guys handling your quarantine?" she wanted to know.

He shrugged. "You know: it's your basic sieve," he said. "But we're doing what we can to keep it going."

He tipped his head toward hers and sat quietly with her, and it made her feel a little better. They stayed like that for some minutes, listening to the sounds of her mother cleaning up downstairs.

"I should get going; you probably have an early shift tomorrow," he finally said, and she gave him a smile.

After a minute he pocketed his phone and got to his feet, and she got up and followed him downstairs to the door. He thanked her mother for having had him over, and she thanked him for coming, and Val followed him outside and put her hand on his shoulder and told him she'd see him soon. "You rode your bike here?" she asked.

"Exercise," he said. He pulled some lights from his pannier and Velcroed one around his bicep and snapped the other into a mount on his handlebars and switched them both on. Once they started flashing, he looked pleased with his accessories, and swung the bike around onto the street, straddled it, and rode away.

"He seems pretty good," her mother said when Val came back into the house. Val nodded and said she was hitting the hay. She fell asleep almost as soon as she climbed into bed, and she woke up coughing and headachy and sick, her sheets soaked with sweat.

"No no no no no," she told herself, only half awake but petrified, and she stepped into the shower and scrubbed herself down, as if that was all she needed to do, and she turned up the heat for the steam, and still found that she had more and more trouble breathing, and she was still saying no to herself while she toweled down and climbed into her sweatshirt and back into bed, and pulled the covers up to her face, and then just went blank, waiting for the sun.

VII

✳ ✳ ✳ ✳ ✳ ✳ ✳ ✤ ✳ ✳ ✳ ✳ ✳ ✳ ✳ ✳ ✳ ✳ ✳

Ililussat went without power for two days, and toward the end of the second day, the hospital had a temporary blackout as well when the diesel generators ran dry. Portable backups kicked in for the life support and HEPA machines, but in the midst of it Danice texted Jeannine *Sitting in the dark in Greenland.* Some lights and heat were jerry-rigged by a custodial guy everyone called Kleivan, who, when he was working in the converted storeroom Danice had been using, seemed to have a plumber's resourcefulness when it came to both improvising tools and coming up with strategies for bypassing problems.

The wards were still packed. Another row of cargo containers had been hauled in out back and the maternity ward had been decommissioned as a mortuary and turned into another isolation room with another HEPA machine flown in from Denmark.

There hadn't been any fresh food in three days and they'd been living on shipments of Danish army rations. Along with the usual precautions, Danice continually washed her hands with Betadine and used hand sanitizers and tried not to touch her eyes, nose, or mouth. She also tried to spend fewer nights wide awake and obsessing about things she couldn't do anything about, but that was easier said than done.

The bad news was that Marie Louisa remained too sick to work, but the good news was that otherwise she seemed to have stabilized. Danice visited her often enough in isolation that Marie Louisa joked whenever she saw Danice coming, "Oh, *some*one needs more advice." Marie Louisa's assistant had gotten only marginally better at overcoming her panic and doing her job, and had developed the habit of snatching up her tea mug and disappearing whenever Danice needed something. As Jeannine's replacement Jerry Sussman had turned out to be amiable and hardworking and smart, but his attempts to demonstrate his language skills in his first few meetings had caused most of the medical staff to exchange glances.

"I guess my Danish is a little rusty," he'd apologized on his first day.

"I would call it *intermittent*," Dr. Hammekin had told him. Hammekin had, with the deaths of Drs. Kristensen and Holm, taken over as head administrator. His English was good and he was cordial to Jerry but he had seemed to stop engaging Danice. It had gotten to the point that when she spoke to him he answered Jerry. She'd finally asked him what his problem was, and it had turned out that Olsen had been one of his prized students and best friends, and that he hadn't forgiven Danice and Jeannine for having gotten Olsen sick.

Since Jerry was the epi and Danice the MD, she was the one who gave Hammekin a hand every morning with the new arrivals. No one was worried about attending privileges when things got this apocalyptic. But of course it meant a much higher risk factor, as Jeannine pointed out to her on the phone. Danice and Hammekin wore masks and gloves and eye shields and the first day they'd worked together someone had sneezed right in Hammekin's face. Intake was two long tables next to the front door, and two rows of folding chairs for those waiting. On one an old woman sat with her hands pressed to her belly. Next to her a father kept his arm around a small son, and behind them against the wall was a whole family, with a teenager who seemed to be trying to sleep across three chairs, his head hanging off one side and his feet the other.

Marie Louisa's assistant briefed Hammekin on how many new beds had opened up and midsentence she switched to Danish and they continued the conversation. It turned out that the family spoke English, so Danice dealt with them at the other end of one of the tables. The teenager roused himself and sat up, raking his hair back and forth with his fingers. They were all sick, and panicked, and she tried to reassure them as much as she could and then asked them to describe their experiences of the illness, and then who had gotten sick first and how, whether they'd had any unusual contact with animals or travelers, whether they'd visited anywhere new. She asked if there was anyone sick who hadn't come in with them, and the mother said no, but one of the daughters immediately looked down and away, and when Danice said, "Who's still sick at home?" the daughter said her grandmother.

The mother said a number of their neighbors were concealing their symptoms, too, and the father agreed and said that his uncle had died without even trying to see his nearest relations because he hadn't wanted to infect them.

Two more families came in, and Danice, with Marie Louisa's assistant translating, got their information as well, and then she found spots for all three families wedged into the new isolation room, and then had to take a break and wandered outside and around to the back of the hospital and pulled off her mask and eye shield.

The sun was arriving earlier each morning. Inside a picket fence someone had set up a little grill on a table where the rock dropped away with a view of the cove's icebergs. Out beyond them the battered orange-and-white regional ferry was still running. Seabirds she couldn't identify sideslipped back and forth over its wake. The narrow bridge over the gorge had the town's name on its railings in big blue metal letters. Some front loaders carrying more cargo containers were heading up onto it and didn't even rouse the sleeping dogs they passed on the side of the road. She could smell the brine and marine life and the diesel.

Hammekin had come up behind her and was blowing his cigarette smoke in her direction. His mask was down around his neck like a cravat. Between the church and the old people's home off to their left, two tiny boys were playing the world's worst game of badminton over a sagging net while waving off mosquitoes.

Hammekin told her that three more of the hospital volunteers had refused to report and seemed to have made off with a crate of rations as well, like the other workers. Supposedly they'd barricaded themselves in with their supplies.

"What do you call chaos once it's gone on forever?" he wondered.

"Normal?" Danice suggested.

"You really have to cover your mouth when you cough," he told her.

"Sorry," she said. "I thought I had."

Down below the bridge, the windshields of the fishing boats periodically blinded her with reflected sunlight. "Did Dr. Olsen have an extended family?" she asked.

He didn't answer. With each wave in the harbor, the boats' mooring lines slapped the water.

"That Kleivan is a magic man," she finally added. "Where would we be without him?"

"This *is* a big country for duct tape," Hammekin told her. "People up here are used to having to make things work however they can."

One of the badminton boys missed the shuttlecock yet again and fell into the net, pulling it down.

"Maybe we should get Kleivan on the job, in terms of identifying what this thing is," Danice said.

"Some of us have thought of that," Hammekin said. It didn't feel like a joke they were sharing, and while she watched the boy untangle himself from the net, Hammekin turned and went back inside.

THE TRACK OF THE INVISIBLE MAN

Even deciding on which people to quarantine wasn't that simple, given the banality of the initial symptoms, and the ridiculousness of the squeeze in terms of available space. Information sharing was nonstop from Greenland to Atlanta to Porton Down to WHO headquarters to Rocky Mountain Labs to Fort Detrick to any number of other places, and still no one had much of anything yet, and no one was even sure of that.

Talent and hard work got you a certain distance, but then you still needed luck. But it seemed to Danice and to everybody with whom she consulted all over the world that every third clue introduced a confounder, an element that seemed to drive the investigation off track. And each pattern that was initially found significant devolved into a maddening knot of ambiguities. Whenever Danice thought she'd spotted something, it started to look more like the result of some other factor. You couldn't go all in on any observation but couldn't let one go, either. Everyone was working the problem, but people had to be thinking that she was *right there, on the ground, where it started:* maybe she'd *missed* something?

Jerry had brought a number of pads of Post-it notes as his way of keeping track of random notions, and they were stuck everywhere around their workstations. There was also in one big plastic bin a knee-high heap of empty Faxe Kondi cans, the only soft drink left in the vending machines. Danice hated the taste of it but kept drinking it anyway.

It felt like every half hour she pushed back from her computer and put her hands over her eyes. It was getting harder and harder, with everything else going on, to just sit in front of it hour after hour, entering data and fielding incoming messages as if she had all the time in the world. She was tired of doing endless work that was intricate and tedious, and tired of being tired.

She could feel a breeze on her butt. In one of the rooms in which they'd lost three people in a row they'd used so much bleach in the cleanup that when she'd leaned against the table the residue had eaten a hole in her pants.

"It's all this pressure and feeling like there's been no progress," she said to Jerry, by way of explaining having sat there inert for some minutes while he pattered away on his keyboard.

"Welcome to the Epidemic Intelligence Service," he told her. He reminded her that EIS veterans always claimed that the letters stood for "Everyday I Sit."

"You know what the definition of *investigate* is?" he asked. When she shook her head, he answered, " 'To flounder.' "

"In our case, that's generous," she said, unencouraged.

A virus would explain why antibiotics had been no help, and there'd been a number of viruses that had turned up among the infected, but those viruses normally should not have been a problem, or at least not *the* problem. They looked to be just non-pathogenic passengers. It was possible something overlooked was working synergistically with something else to produce the disease, even if otherwise incapable of producing it on its own, and everybody knew that old viruses could cause new syndromes in new circumstances. It was possible that something was mutating more prolifically or rapidly than anyone might have expected, or that there was some kind of gene swapping going on that they were missing. She remembered something the head of WHO had said a decade or so earlier in a speech, even before COVID, about what happened if you left a burglar in front of a locked door with a sack of random keys and gave him enough time.

The thing didn't even need to be new. It might be something that had been around forever and had needed only a minimal genomic change to arrange its route past our immune systems.

Jerry reminded her that for years the Eaton agent that had been associated with cold agglutinin-positive pneumonia, a version of cold agglutinin disease, or CAD, had been assumed to be a virus, but then they'd been able to grow it on cell-free artificial media, and it had turned out to be a mycoplasma that was crucially different from other members of its genus.

"So how do you find the invisible man?" Danice wondered aloud. She cracked open another can of Faxe Kondi and looked glumly at what she was about to drink.

Jerry shrugged. "Look in the snow?" he suggested. "Wait for it to rain?"

"And what happens when you can't wait?" she wanted to know. Earlier that afternoon, Marie Louisa's fever had started yo-yoing again, and had gotten as high as 105.

He reminded her that the EIS's symbol was the fouled anchor, for a boat in trouble, crossed with a caduceus. And that the worldwide symbol of the field epidemiologist was a hole in the sole of a shoe.

"Have you noticed how often you tell me stuff I already know?" Danice remarked.

Jerry smiled. "I find that anything that sounds like a dad joke keeps up morale," he told her.

She was going to give him more grief, but he meant well, and she was too tired even for sarcasm, so she let it go.

She had nightmares that night, and before she'd even settled into her workstation with her coffee the next morning, Jerry reported that now Atlanta, on top of everything else, wanted them to do some public relations work.

"Well, to be fair, I think it's more important than I just made it sound," he said, when he saw her face.

It turned out that the president had authorized with a special directive the forming of an Epidemic Emergency Interagency Working Group, with representatives from the CDC, the NIH, the DOD, and the State Department, with liaisons to WHO and UN Disaster Relief, and that that entire brain trust had gotten together and had produced as one of its first initiatives the notion that they needed all hands on deck to get on the same page in terms of the information that was going out.

Governments had their hands full directing their first responders and working to support their health care organizations and tracking exposures, but in most countries the nonmedical effects of the outbreak were draining a greater and greater proportion of resources as well, and many of those effects were being driven by the kind of misinformation they could do more to combat. There needed to be more widespread compliance with the medical recommendations being issued, and the Interagency Working Group was proposing as a first step what it called an "Information Inoculation" to combat the increasing impression that official sources were not to be trusted.

"Well, what do they want *us* to do about it?" Danice wanted to know.

"Read it yourself," Jerry said, his hand out to the computer screen.

The bottom line was that the government was certain it needed to do better at getting its messages across clearly and credibly, and that media professionals who had been recruited from the private sector would soon be in touch as to how the CDC's team in Ililussat could contribute to any number of public information materials—from Instagram posts to tweets to YouTube videos to Wikipedia pages to podcasts—targeted for various demographics. As the country's representatives in the place where most people assumed this whole thing had started, they were uniquely situated when it came to the battle for attention and claims of authority.

"*Pod*casts?" Danice exclaimed.

"I think what they want are just a few things from us that they can spread around social media," Jerry ventured. "I'm not sure what we can say that would *reassure* anybody, but they'd clearly like us to give it a shot."

"Do they think we're not *overwhelmed* here?" Danice asked. "In terms of time?"

"When we get a minute," Jerry said. "*If* we get a minute."

"I'm going to go see what's happening with intake," she told him. "Then I'll be back."

"Top-down messaging has stopped working," he added as she got her things together. "People are saying that agency heads are serving their own agendas. Apparently the hope is that heroic grunts like you and me in the front lines will be seen differently."

"I can't hear you," she said, once she was out in the hall.

"And there were a few countries that went way too long denying their outbreaks," he called after her. "So everybody's dealing with that blowback as well."

THIS IS NORMAL

She was hunting up some Zofran for a ten-year-old who'd thrown up all over the intake table when Jerry texted her a document headed "SOME IDEAS FOR THE MEDIA PEOPLE" and the heading annoyed her so much she stepped outside, but Hammekin and some other medical staffers were having a confab and eyed her, so she ducked back inside and through the closest door, which led her down a flight of concrete steps to the basement.

A few people were coming and going fetching things, but otherwise it was much quieter. The hallway was lit by only a few buzzing ceiling bulbs, and was nose to nose with rolling carts and bins. Her phone buzzed, and it was her mother calling again, and she thought why not, at this point, and answered it.

Her mother when Danice answered always said her name like she was startled to find her on the other end of the line.

"She's all right," her mother said to someone else, probably Danice's brother.

"Is Danny there? How's he doing? How *are* you guys?" Danice asked.

"How're you?" her mother asked. Danny in the background said, "She's all right?" and her mother snapped "What did I *just* say?"

Danice took a breath and rode out the surreality of her mother's voice in this context. "I'm fine. Knock wood," she said. "So everybody's good, Ma?" she asked again.

"We're all fine," her mother said. "Your brother thought it was the end of the world that you weren't answering."

"It's been crazy here," Danice said.

"I can imagine," her mother said. "Hold *on*," she told Danice's brother. "He's so excited to talk to you," she explained. She liked to think of herself as someone who saw the best in him even when he disappointed everyone else.

"How's Grandma?" Danice asked.

"They're going to have to beat her to death with a stick," her mother said. "Last time I talked to her she said she hoped you weren't working on anything dangerous."

Danice chuckled.

"I'll put your brother on in a minute," her mother said. "So *is* anybody there making any progress?"

She told her mother that their joke now was that pretty much whatever they were asked, their answer was always "We don't know, but we're working on it."

"Well, I predict you're going to end up being the big hero in all of this," her mother said.

"I certainly prefer that to what *I've* been predicting," Danice said.

"Well, you tend to think the worst," her mother said.

"I think that's *you* you're thinking of," Danice told her.

"Okay, well, here's your brother. Take care," her mother said.

"Hey hey," her brother said. "You're good?"

"I'm good. And Ma says everybody there is good," Danice said.

"Well," Danny said. "Mrs. Calzolaio died."

The Calzolaios had been their lifelong neighbors. "Ma said everybody there was good," Danice protested.

"Yeah, well," Danny answered.

"Jeez," she complained.

"Ma's been in a kind of circle-the-wagons mode," Danny said. "If you're not family, she doesn't want to know about you."

"Nice," Danice said. "Real Good Samaritan stuff."

"You had Ma pegged as a Good Samaritan?" he asked.

"So what's it like there?" she wanted to know.

"It's like everywhere else," he said. "Most stuff is closed. The only places that are busy are the electronics stores. I guess everyone needs their phones and laptops one way or the other. I been helping out at the school. The National Guard's been handing out water and things people need."

"That's great," Danice said. Then, when he didn't say anything to that, she said, "I'm proud of you."

"Yeah, well, I figured out as a kid that just because someone was ashamed of you that didn't mean you had to be ashamed of yourself," he said.

"She wasn't *ashamed* of you," Danice said.

"So listen," her brother said. "You take care of yourself."

"Of course," she said. "You too."

"We love you," he said. "Everybody's scared shitless here but we love you." He told her to check in when she could, even if it was just a text, and she promised she would, and then the phone got passed back and forth between her brother and mother with each of them having to say goodbye and then remembering something else, and it took another five minutes to get off.

WHO DOESN'T MISS WHAT'S-HER-NAME?

She got off one call and found herself on another when Jeannine's number popped up while she was heading back up the stairs.

"Look who's got a free minute," Danice said when she answered. She stopped and headed back down.

"How're you guys doing?" Jeannine wanted to know. "Everything fall apart there without me to hold it together?" They'd promised they were going to keep each other updated by text, and they had for a little while, but after a week of some pretty basic exchanges, most things other than the trading of information updates had petered out. While they'd been saying goodbye, Danice had predicted it would, and Jeannine had responded, "Why do you always assume that nobody likes you?"

"There's a whole new sheriff in town," Danice told her. "Your replacement keeps going, 'Who decided to do things *this* way?' "

"So is Sussman wowing everybody with his Danish?" Jeannine wanted to know.

"His Danish is about as good as my singing," Danice said.

"So really, how *are* things going there?" Jeannine asked.

Danice caught her up. There'd been some problem with the hotel so they'd moved her to a two-room house closer to the harbor. It was bolted to the rock and uninsulated and had no running water. Snow that was tracked in never melted. Her neighbor was a woman who everybody said had shot her first husband when he hadn't gotten the things she wanted at the store. Outside her house she had a whale rib stuck upright in the sand. And things were bad enough now that people had stopped coming to the weekend open-air markets. The day before she'd seen a woman pass someone lying on the street without checking to see if the guy was okay.

"So what's it like there?" Danice finally said. "How's it working in a Level 4?"

Jeannine said that she lived across the street from the lab and that even so it took her three full hours to get to the point where she could start her work. She said that the security was out of this world, and that they were a long way from the old days when a mailman could walk into a smallpox lab to deliver a package. She said she'd never realized what it would be like to work day after day in one of those suits. She said that after the first day you learned not to have a coffee first or to go in feeling hungry. The negative airflow dehydrated you faster than you'd think, so most people didn't stick it out much past three hours. And the suit was heavy. You really felt it on your shoulders. And there was nothing worse than getting something like a runny nose. You couldn't blow it, so people got creative with towels and kerchiefs around their necks and stuff like that. And if you did sneeze, you couldn't clean your face shield. She said that everyone told her that an hour in there was like three in a high-stress environment in the real world, so nearly everyone burned out after five or six years, or way sooner, after their first near accident.

"If you're trying to impress me, so far I don't see the excitement here," Danice told her.

It was mostly a matter of training and concentration, Jeannine said. It was probably like being a cop or a firefighter in that you just practiced everything until you got so you could handle dangerous situations smoothly. And anyway, because it was so hard working in the suits, they tried to do as much as possible on components of whatever they were working on that had been inactivated and could be moved down to Level 2 labs. But of course they had to identify something before they could do that in this case.

"Long hours?" Danice commiserated.

"I've seen so little of the sun I feel like a miner," Jeannine complained.

"What're the people like?" Danice asked. "Is there anybody there as fun as me?"

"Is there anybody anywhere as fun as you?" Jeannine asked. She said she liked the chief of virology, Hank. He sang songs from *Hamilton* when he was suited up, and he loved that everybody else had to listen on their earpieces.

"Hank Feldman? I've heard of him," Danice said.

"He's always touring everybody's labs to see what people need and what he can do to help," Jeannine told her. She said he had this knack for getting people who were already totally committed to work even harder, and it reminded her of the way her dad used to tease her that most opportunities were missed because they showed up looking like work. She said that whenever there was anything like encouraging news, Hank said to everyone around him in a singsong voice, "Well, maybe something is going on." And that he always pulled the most relevant piece of information from whatever you put in front of him. "He's also always saying that if we're not wrong half the time, we're not being brave enough," Jeannine added.

"Well, we're plenty brave here, then," Danice told her.

Jeannine snorted. She had a way of snorting at the end of her laughs that always made Danice laugh.

"I made Hank laugh the first day," Jeannine told her. "He was going on about how he wanted his labs to be the kind of places where people could be proud to say 'I don't know.' And then he asked me this really basic question, and I was like, 'I don't know.'"

"I'm jealous," Danice said.

"I think he could've been a member of the Junior Certain Death Squad," Jeannine said.

"I thought that was just us," Danice said.

"A junior member," Jeannine said. When Danice let it go at that, she added, "So how're you doing otherwise?"

Danice told her that most of the time she was so tired, she worried that the possibility of insight was out the window, and she was just doing data management.

"No, I mean otherwise," Jeannine said. "With the rest of everything."

"Oh, you know me," Danice told her. "I'm just sitting here on OkCupid."

Jeannine chuckled. "You ever do one of those things?" she wanted to know.

"Once, and then I had to get off the site," Danice told her. "I get scared looking at an endless menu of guys." When Jeannine chuckled again, Danice added that it used to be that you had to do a little work to get yourself into trouble. And that she still remembered when that kind of dating service was for the saddest kind of losers.

"So listen," Jeannine said. "Whatever happened with the burial stuff? Can I tell the kid that it's all taken care of?"

"It's all taken care of," Danice confirmed. "You need me to send photos of the plots?"

"You'd better," Jeannine said. "I'm not sure he's taking *my* word for anything."

They were quiet. "You know, I wanted to call anyway," Jeannine said. "To see how you were doing."

"Sure," Danice said. "So." They were quiet again. "How about you? Have you been taking care of yourself?"

"Oh, I'm fine," Jeannine said. "Besides living on chai lattes. And I've been eating so many Sun Chips I probably should just apply them directly to my butt."

"So how's the kid?" Danice said.

"About how you'd expect," Jeannine said. "Did I tell you I'm actually bringing Branislav here to help out with him?"

"*Bran*islav?" Danice said. "No, you didn't."

"He's about as well qualified for this as anybody," Jeannine argued. "And what're you snorting about?"

"I'm not snorting about anything," Danice said.

There was a buzzing on the line, and then it went away. "*Bran-islav*," Danice said again.

"He's pretty amazing when it comes to getting through to kids," Jeannine said.

"Well, here's hoping he comes through for everybody," Danice said.

They each waited for the other to offer something else. "I miss you," Jeannine finally added.

"I just talked to my mom," Danice told her. "She said she predicts that I'm going to end up being the big hero in all of this."

"Ha. That's my prediction, too," Jeannine agreed.

"I think it's going to be you," Danice said.

"Oh, I doubt that," Jeannine murmured. Danice could hear an increase of noise from the floor above in the hospital, like a group had just poured into the intake area.

"I had this real hardass for a tutorial in grad school," Jeannine finally said. "And this one time when I told him that maybe my project hadn't panned out because it had been too ambitious, he said that he'd always thought that the moral of the Icarus story was not 'Don't try to fly too high.' He said he thought it was 'Do a better job on the wings.'"

The door above the stairs swung open with a bang, startling Danice. "If you're finished with your day on the phone," Jerry told her, "there are one or two other things around here that could use your attention."

She held up her hand for him and told Jeannine that she had to get off, and Jeannine agreed that she had to get off, too, and they promised to stay in touch. And Danice came upstairs into the bright light of the lobby, and sat at one of the intake tables and apologized to Jerry and Dr. Hammekin, and started working with a nurse to take down information, but Jerry didn't seem mollified, and after a few minutes he got up and left, and she didn't see him again for the rest of the morning.

VIII

�֍ �֍ �֍ �֍ ✖ ╬ ✖ ✖ ✖ ✖ ✖ ✖ ✖ ✖ ✖ ✖

A disease outbreak spreading rapidly among a large number of patients within a single region is considered an epidemic, from the Greek for "upon the people," and that same outbreak spread to a certain number of other geographic regions is classified as a pandemic, from the Greek "for all people."

Those definitions had now also spread worldwide. The billions of texts, tweets, photos, videos, and other postings tsunami-ing in all directions in response to the general panic featured some helpful information, the way in negotiating a nearly impenetrable rain forest you might every so often come across an edible piece of fruit. The good news was that the internet democratized and facilitated the sharing of information, and that was the bad news, as well. All of those media platforms that served as back channels in the information universe now overwhelmed official channels, and overwhelmed themselves, as well; servers crashed and spikes in capacity never receded. Data centers reported continual extended network and power outages, and new spikes appeared with each new rumor. People claiming they already had vaccines were everywhere, as were people who claimed to have stumbled across other preventatives. One influencer from Australia who before the pandemic had hit had been sponsored by various upscale home and bath product companies and had made her family's affluence look like a permanent vacation was now announcing that her family had been kept safe by an elaborate and fanatically precise diet and hygiene regimen. She had gone from five million to forty-five million followers on Instagram. On the one hand, useful information might have been pouring in from everywhere; on the other, you had to stir through the stew of journalism and entertainment and horseshit and noise to find it. And anything was probably more comforting than the official story, which seemed perpetually to be "We're working on it," and with so many more appealing options out there reality was being abandoned the way you might walk away from farmland that had lost its water source.

In the mornings before she went in to work, Jeannine gave herself ten minutes while she had her coffee to catch herself up and bring herself down when it came to all of this. Postings about a run on clarithromycin had generated pharmacy riots in seven cities in the South and Midwest. Why only the South and Midwest, no one could say. There was a robust black market for high-filtration masks. With China's lockdown, supply chains were breaking down all over Europe and North America, and even the most basic prescription drugs were disappearing. The COVID-19 pandemic had exposed the way America's health care system, having been stripped to the bare bones to maximize profit, was uniquely ill-equipped to handle the dramatically added burdens of disaster. But as in so many instances in American politics, after the lesson had been learned nothing had been done about it. One frustrated CDC media liaison had been shitcanned after, in response to a question by a CNN reporter about what government could be doing differently, he suggested an immediate halt to all flights out of states with Republican governors to reduce the spread of political imbecility. Videos of people trying to get out of their cities by highway or airport had caused a stampede of others to do the same. Images of airports and train stations during the first few weeks had looked like the fall of Saigon; now, with the lockdowns in place, pictures of empty spaces circled the world: no one in Times Square; one woman facing the vast colonnade outside St. Peter's. Whole sections of store shelves had been cleared out and truckers were refusing to haul freight to some regions. Nurses and nurses' aides were refusing to work and rebelling at being thrown into the fire with no real plan for how to save either them or their patients. Hospitals in hotspots were rationing care of all kinds. Amazon was unable to ship and had turned its flywheels to the problem, and Alexa could now list for customers in real time where riots were occurring, which hospitals were shut down, where to locate updates on the CDC's website, how to find the safest noninfected areas within various preset radii, and which homeopathic remedies were trending. Google was tracking pneumonia activity by analyzing the changing numbers of requests for information on the subject and cross-referencing those requests with their geographic locations. A 737 in Chicago had been disabled on the tarmac by a passenger riot when its Wi-Fi had gone down and an emergency exit was opened and didn't reseal when closed.

Jeannine sent that last link to Branislav, whose first day was today. She texted underneath it that for most people the worst news probably wasn't so much the collapse of order and infrastructure as it was the possibility that the party was over. No free Wi-Fi, she wrote— *that* was when the survivors were going to envy the dead. Branislav didn't text back.

Her father texted that he'd heard that people in China were being cured with something called dioscorea root, and wanted to know if she'd heard about that, and if they were looking into it where she was. She began a response and then found herself just staring at his words. All those people out there, spreading anything they wanted, out of desperation or for recreation or for no reason at all. Maybe democracy worked for restaurant reviews and movie ratings, but boy, was it creating problems in this case. What were all those dystopias she'd had to read about in high school, concerning the individual trampled by the state, talking about? Why hadn't anyone imagined the chaos of *no* one in charge?

She still hadn't answered the questions Hank had forwarded her from an epidemiologist at the WHO in Geneva about Aleq. They didn't much prioritize the WHO's communications in general, since it was always running on a shoestring, with an annual budget less than that of a decent-sized city hospital. Its viral unit in Geneva was six people, three of whom had allegedly been hired for administrative work. Three real virologists and a board of like 190 ministers, all political appointees. That, too, was supposed to have changed after COVID and hadn't. And like the CDC, between disasters the WHO was always having to sit still for "realistic" administrative reviews that further shaved its budget.

The rule of thumb for most elected officials was that they worked tirelessly to make things worse. In the U.S., whichever party was in power wasn't interested in support for public health. Public health never competed well for resources in either the House or the Senate. Countries were like people: they didn't value health until they lost it. And then once they got it back, they returned to their old complacency.

A lot of media outlets were calling the illness "RAS," now, for Respiratory Arrest Syndrome, and there was a term, RAS Orphans, for people who had lost their entire families. Around the lab, nobody mentioned myxomatosis, and nobody had to. After rabbits had been introduced to Australia in the nineteenth century as a food source, by 1950 their populations had gotten so out of hand that microbiologists had been encouraged to introduce a virus from a Brazilian rabbit against which the Australian rabbits would have had no defenses. The result had been a successful manmade extinction experiment: within three months, 99.8 percent of the rabbit population of the entire southeast of Australia—a land area larger than Western Europe—had been eradicated. The good news, epidemiologists liked to say when they did talk about it, was that eventually the lethality rate had diminished, so that after seven years, it had gotten down to 25 percent.

IX

✦ ✦ ✦ ✦ ✦ ✦ ✦ ✝ ✦ ✦ ✦ ✦ ✦ ✦ ✦ ✦ ✦ ✦ ✦

The BSL-4 cube had windows to allow workers inside to look across the atrium at the BSL-2 labs, and vice versa, so at any point during their sessions Branislav not only had the Zoom option on his monitor but could also look over and see Aleq's entire room and Jeannine as well. She waved.

Through the next window over, he could see a technician weighing mice. Jeannine had informed him, when giving him a much more comprehensive tour of the facility than he required, that the animal procedure and holding rooms were next to the patient rooms down the main hallway, and featured not only HEPA-filtered cages but MRIs for noninvasive means of tracking whatever pathogenesis might be going on.

Both Hank and Emily were dubious about how much could be accomplished with a tablet screen in terms of getting through to someone, especially a traumatized child, but as Hank put it, so what? They weren't social workers or psychologists.

"I would think it'd be hard enough face-to-face," Hank had added in their initial meeting when Jeannine had been showing Branislav around.

It was like giving someone a hug with salad tongs, Branislav had agreed, having done his share of it. He wasn't a big fan of telehealth, but it was here to stay.

The translator sat beside him and there was a half-second delay with the earpiece, which didn't help matters. They'd told him the Wi-Fi was likely to be problematic sometimes as well, but so far it seemed okay.

Once the video feed was on and they were both centered in each other's view, Jeannine did the introductions, and Branislav said hello. Aleq didn't answer. When the boy finally spoke, Branislav could hear the despair in his voice before the translation even came through. It turned out he was asking about the burial of his friend and relatives. Jeannine reassured him that all of that had taken place as she'd promised, and while Branislav waited, she showed him some photos as proof. He asked where his grandparents and friend had been put in the cemetery, and she showed him some additional photos from farther away and pointed out the locations. He asked if his parents had been put nearby and she pointed out their graves as well.

He asked to hold the tablet, and Jeannine handed it over, and waited while he studied the pictures. The tablet was covered with a clear plastic and would stay in the room. After what she apparently estimated to be a sufficient amount of time, she introduced Branislav again, and clicked the Zoom window to make it the primary one. Branislav said hello again and told Aleq that he was here to answer any questions, and that he worked with kids to help them feel better about whatever was making them sad or scared.

Aleq didn't respond, but Branislav hadn't thought he would. Then the boy pulled the earpiece from his ear and tossed it on the bed, and let the tablet drop, and Branislav found himself looking up at the overhead lights. Through the window he could see Aleq lying back, and Jeannine leaning over him, maybe putting the earpiece back in his ear.

"It's always the first appointment of the day," Branislav murmured.

Aleq came back onscreen, so Jeannine must have righted the tablet.

"Show him the box," Branislav told her. He'd given her a box of toys to take in with her, and she brought it over to Aleq and held the tablet while he peered inside. After a minute he pulled out some kind of action hero in a blue superhero outfit. It had a lever on its back that made its arm punch and leg kick, and he started the arm punching and the leg kicking and kept both going while Jeannine explained to him that she and Branislav just wanted to talk with him for a little while, and to see if he had questions they could help him with.

"Show him the hourglass," Branislav told her, and she dug the plastic hourglass from a board game out of the box and held it in front of the boy. Branislav told her to flip it over and then told Aleq that when all the sand had gone to the bottom they'd be finished talking for today.

Aleq seemed uninterested in the hourglass and instead said something slowly to Jeannine, like he wanted to make sure she caught every word. "He says to thank you for what you did about burying everybody," the translator told them.

Jeannine seemed momentarily at a loss, and Branislav told her to move the tablet's camera lens even closer to Aleq. He instructed her to move the lens around right up next to Aleq's face, and then down his body. The boy shied backward a little and Branislav said, "Um-hmmmm: I *see*," like the Wise Doctor who'd discovered the problem, and even Aleq picked up on his tone and gave him back the trace of a smile after the translator finished.

"Do you *have* any questions?" Branislav asked him, but Aleq closed his eyes and pretended to be asleep. Branislav asked if he was tired, but got no answer. They waited each other out for a few minutes, and Branislav looked over into the room through the window, and even from that distance he could see Jeannine giving him a look meant to communicate *Well, do something*. After another five minutes, he told her to put a blanket over Aleq. She pulled one up to the boy's chin. On the screen he watched Aleq breathe. He told Jeannine to tell him when the sand ran out. After another eight minutes, she told him it had.

"All right, that's it for today," he said.

"We're finished?" she asked.

"For today," he told her.

"You gotta be kidding me," she said.

"It's his trip," Branislav told her. "I'm just the witness."

"This is kind of urgent, what we're trying to find out," she said.

"There's a limit to how much you can rush this," he said. "And maybe we should cut him a little slack. He's just been looking at his parents' graves."

Afterward they ran into Hank in the atrium café.

"How'd it go?" Hank asked.

Jeannine held her hand out for Branislav to speak.

"Fine," he told Hank. "I thought he did exactly what he needed to do."

"That's good to hear," Hank said. And then, after a pause, he asked, "What was it he needed to do?"

Again Jeannine held out her hand to Branislav, and he smiled and said, "You know. Rest. Recharge. Begin that whole process of starting to sound things out with us."

"Ah," Hank said. And then he looked at them both, and let it go at that.

FAILURE TO THRIVE

Branislav agreed by text to review their first session that night in her apartment. When he got there she asked if he wanted some wine and he said no, and she asked if he wanted some tea and he said no to that, too.

She thought about pouring a little wine for herself and then closed the refrigerator door. "Well, let's get down to it, then," she said, and sat at her kitchen island.

"Did you pick this place?" he asked, sitting opposite her and looking around. He was wearing the same plain V-neck white T-shirt he'd been wearing that afternoon.

"You get assigned a place," she told him. He pulled some notebooks and his phone out of a saddlebag she remembered, and then leaned forward on the countertop with both hands, like he was about to get to his feet again, but, given his expression, he was apparently just stretching. He wasn't that big, but he somehow always gave the impression of being barrel-chested.

"So what do you think?" she asked.

He walked her through his observations. The first was that Aleq had eye tics, and Branislav thought they were from stress.

"I hadn't noticed that," she said, and then hated herself when she registered his reaction. Given their history, he probably thought she should have that phrase on a sign around her neck.

When she felt the silence grow awkward enough, she couldn't stop herself from adding, "So why'd you give up so easily this morning?"

He regarded her from across the counter and then said that a lot of the time it was about being willing to have enough patience to allow the child to make his own sense out of the situations that might be overwhelming to him.

"So it's about waiting the kid out?" she asked.

Who knew what Aleq had seen, or lived through, Branislav told her. She'd given him the outline, but imagine the particulars. "I mean, I've seen what it does to kids just to be removed and placed," he said. That was what they called it when someone had to be taken out of their home: "removed and placed." "Imagine what it must be like to watch your whole home wiped out," he added. "And then on top of that to wonder if maybe you were responsible."

"I've told him that he shouldn't think it was his fault," she said. "That he may not have infected anyone." How much truth did somebody in his position need, anyhow? she added.

"I usually haven't regretted telling kids the truth," Branislav told her.

"He's really just been barely holding it together," Jeannine said.

With a lot of the smaller kids, the diagnosis that got somebody like himself pulled in was failure to thrive, Branislav told her. Aleq reminded him of one of those kids.

Aleq had been doing a little better lately, Jeannine reported. He'd answered a few questions during one or two sessions but then he had clammed up again.

It was about getting him to trust, Branislav said, by showing him certain things about the way they were willing to be with him.

"What kind of things?" Jeannine asked. "What have you shown him?"

He looked at her as if to say, *You were* there *this morning.* "That I'll wait for him to signal a willingness to interact before I'll push any harder. That I'll play a part in whatever story he does decide to begin. And that I'm willing to start in the dark."

She made a noise. It probably sounded impatient.

"He'll start answering when he's ready," Branislav finally said.

"Or else he won't," she told him back.

"Or else he won't," he agreed.

"So I guess we just have to have faith," she told him.

"A mother once told me that I was going to help her kid, and that she could *see* it," he said. "I remember I told her that I was glad *she* could. Because *I* sure couldn't."

"So should I have any reason for optimism?" she asked.

"When I was Aleq's age I was so shy when I got called on in school, I got through it by counting the seconds until the teacher moved on to somebody else. I just ignored what I was being asked and stared straight ahead and counted. At one point they brought my parents in, because they thought I was having seizures or something."

"So you may be uniquely suited to drawing Aleq out, is the idea here," she ventured.

He shrugged. They were trying to build a little bit of intimacy as quickly as they could, he explained, and for that they'd need the boy to feel both like he had some privacy, and that he was safe. "And good luck with both of those where he is," he added.

"The problem is, I'm not sure we can wait for him to be cured of everything he's dealing with," Jeannine told him.

"And we can't wait because . . . ?" Branislav asked.

"If there's another line of transmission—another group of people infected with something else—there could be an entire other population that needs to be contained. In that case every hour would count," Jeannine said.

"Well, that explains that," Branislav answered, making a face at her impatience. "But only hams get cured. And who knows what kind of ground this kid has already gained, and lost.

"I'm sorry I can't provide any guarantees," he added, when he saw her expression.

"No, I know," she said. She blew out a huge breath.

"Sometimes it works out," he told her. He stood and packed everything up. "And sometimes you just pick up your paycheck and go home."

ANOTHER TURN AT THE PIÑATA

The next morning Aleq held his action figure up and made welcoming kicking and punching moves with its legs and arms when Jeannine came through the door.

"Hello to you too," she told him. "He seems in a good mood today," she remarked to Branislav.

"Another turn at the piñata," he told her.

She put her gloved hand to her suit helmet as if she could press the earpiece to her ear. "What kind of joke is *that*?" she said.

"Professional humor," he apologized.

"Don't translate that, Elias," she told the translator.

"I wouldn't even know how," the translator told her.

"Turn the hourglass over where he can see it," Branislav told Jeannine. She found it and turned it over while Aleq watched, and then brought the tablet over and activated the Zoom link.

"How did you hurt your lip?" Branislav asked him.

Aleq waited out the translation and then answered. The translator said, "He says he hit it."

"How did you hit it?" Branislav wanted to know. Aleq didn't answer.

Aleq said something else and the translator said, "He says today you should cover him up."

"What does he mean? With the blanket?" Branislav wanted to know. The translator asked Aleq and then said yes, so Jeannine got the blanket from the foot of the bed and covered him with it. Aleq arranged the action figure so he was just peeking over the covers.

"Give him the animal crackers," Branislav told Jeannine, and she opened the little box she'd brought in with her and passed it to Aleq. He further arranged the action figure under the covers and took the box of cookies and pulled out a bear and looked at it. On the screen, Branislav rooted around in his box, and found a bear as well. He bit the nose off and held the rest in front of him. "Now it's a bear without a nose," he said, and the translator translated.

Aleq waited out the translation and then bit the nose off his.

Branislav took another small bite, and said that now it was a bear without a head. Aleq did the same. Branislav took another bite, and said that now it was a bear without a butt. When the translator translated, Aleq laughed, and Jeannine thought, *I've never heard him laugh*. Branislav ate the last piece and showed his empty hands and exclaimed, "Now there's *no* bear!" and Aleq after the translation laughed again, and did the same.

Aleq asked if he could go to the bathroom. There was a little bathroom in the room. They said sure, and he got out of bed and crossed to it and closed the door behind him. When he returned, he climbed back into bed and pointed to the tablet and said something to Branislav and the translator said, "He says he's been watching snowboarding videos."

"Which ones has he liked?" Branislav asked, and Aleq described three. It was by far the longest Jeannine had ever heard him speak. When he finally finished, there was something else he clearly wanted to say, and after he added it, the translator said, "He wants to know if he can get a hat like the one he saw in the third video."

"I think he can," Branislav said, as if to everyone.

Jeannine could see how pleased the boy was with the answer, even if he didn't smile, and thought it was possible that she could see him trying to come to terms with the idea that maybe this was his life now.

Branislav asked him two more questions about the videos, and Aleq answered the first, and then pointed at the hourglass, where the sand had run out.

"Fair enough. Tell him we'll see him tomorrow," Branislav said, and Jeannine again had to fight back her impatience while she watched the exchange before she headed out of the room.

ANOTHER TURN AT THE PIÑATA

She invited Branislav over that night for some frozen tacos she'd
managed to find, and he said he couldn't make it, so after she'd made
the tacos and eaten two and put the rest away, she sat in her empty
living room for a while, and then went over to the hotel where they
were putting him up.

"Who would've guessed it would be you?" he said after he'd
opened the door and swung it wide so she could enter. A basketball
game was on the television. He gestured to the sofa in front of it and
put the game on mute.

He offered her a beer, and she said sure.

"Are games still going on?" she asked after he'd brought it over and
handed it to her. "They're still playing games?"

"No. This isn't live," he told her. "They're showing old ones."

They watched a few turnovers, and then a scramble for a loose
ball.

"I'd never heard him laugh before," she said. "However many days
we've been together, I'd never heard him laugh."

"He probably didn't have a lot to laugh about," Branislav guessed.

"I think he really likes you," she said. "You know: as much as *I*
can tell anything."

He made a face as if to agree with her.

"It feels like he's doing some healing," she said, almost to herself.
"And that's on you."

He reminded her about the way, in this kind of work, healing was
supposed to be two-sided.

She cracked her beer and sipped it. He waited her out, the way
he'd waited out Aleq.

"He just looks like some part of him is waiting for all those lost
people to come back, even though he knows they're not coming

back," he told her. He took a slug of his beer, and held the can in front of him rather than putting it down.

"How *are* you doing?" she finally asked.

"I seem to be functioning pretty well," he said. "Sometimes I take my own advice."

She nodded, like that was a strategy of which she approved. "I was a little worried after I asked you here, because there are all these ways in which the kid reminds me of Mirko," she said.

He nodded a little, like he'd already been giving that some thought. "Well, it's not like otherwise I would've been fine," he said.

"I'm just sorry to put you through any more than you have to go through," she said.

He turned off the TV like it had started to bother him. "Everything we're selling in this business: it's all some version of 'It's not always your fault,'" he told her.

She teared up, unexpectedly, and then blinked the tears away. They were not only for what he'd been going through, but also for herself. It was like there'd barely been time to recognize what had been amazing about being together, and then it was gone.

"When you're working with someone you want to pretend it's only all about what they're going through," he said. "That's why therapists always sound like they *know* what you need even when they don't."

They drank their beers for a little while. He was looking at the TV as if it had continued to disappoint him even after it had gone off.

"There's so much we never talked about," she finally said, and he sighed. She gave him an apologetic wince when he looked over at her.

"I don't know if *that's* true," he answered.

"I just feel like . . ." she began, and then petered out. "You just should know that you still take up a lot of space in my head."

He let that sit for a minute. "That isn't about me," he said. "That could be just what happens." He thought for a minute, and then added that it was maybe Heidegger who'd noticed that whatever withdrew from us then drew us along by its very withdrawal. "Basic rule of middle school," he said when she didn't say anything in response.

"I mean, in the middle of all of this *I'm* thinking about you," she said.

"It is hard to believe," he commiserated.

"People were like, '*He's* the one you need for this? You really need *him* to work with this kid?'"

"Yeah, that was what I was thinking, too," he said.

"Everyone's probably like, 'Should we have left *her* in charge of this?'" she continued. "'Maybe we should've brought in somebody whiter?'"

He smiled. Their joke when they'd been going out had been that she'd only gotten into graduate school on Algerian affirmative action. She'd confided to him on one of their first nights together that her classmates had always complained to her that she made it look easy, and he had floored her by responding that it probably *had* been easy, once you set aside the eighteen-hour study binges and the weeping and the agonizing and the rage at your own limitations. She had mounted him again, once he'd said that, and had informed him that she wasn't used to being seen with that kind of clarity, and he had put a hand to each of her hips and had said, "You're welcome," and had arched his back so she felt even more filled up by him.

She rubbed her eye, remembering, and finished her beer, thinking how restorative it would be if every so often someone said, *I'd really like to be with you.* "Everybody thought I was crazy to call you and you're probably going to prove that I was right," she said.

"Could be," he said. "Let's see what happens tomorrow."

"Yes. Let's see," she resolved. And she stood up, and bent over, and gave him a little air kiss, and then left.

SOMETIMES EVEN A BLIND SQUIRREL

The next morning Branislav had Jeannine bring Aleq crayons and paper, and Aleq took both and immediately started drawing all over the paper. He explained through the translator that this was how you made a wolf fish, and these were the long lines you set for them, and when he was finished he held it out to Jeannine, and to the tablet lens.

He asked what the date was. After the translator told him, he said, "On June 11th I'll be twelve."

"That's your birthday?" Jeannine asked. In response he did some additional scribbling on the pad.

She sighed so loudly that Branislav said in her earpiece, "Just *give* him a second."

So she stood by the bed and clasped her wrist with her hand as if to mime patience. Aleq drew for another few minutes. When he finished, he kept his attention on the pad, and said something that he seemed to be having trouble putting into words. The translator waited for him to go on, and then said, "He says that sometimes he makes up in his head a picture of his friend Malik remembering him."

Jeannine looked out her window and could see Branislav across the way giving that some thought.

"In the picture Malik is remembering Aleq?" Branislav asked.

The translator passed the question along, and Aleq nodded.

They gave Aleq another minute to draw, and then Branislav asked him what having a picture like that in his head had been like, and Aleq told him that he'd taken that picture and put it in a box, and then put the box in another room, and then put the room in another house.

There was a long enough silence following that that Jeannine figured Branislav had no more idea how to respond than she did. Then Branislav told him that it was okay to have remembered what he remembered and to have forgotten what he forgot, and when Aleq didn't say anything in response, Branislav told him again. It seemed to take the translator longer to translate it the second time.

Aleq returned to his drawing like he needed the privacy. He flipped the page he'd been working on and started something new.

"Do you want any more colors?" Branislav asked him, and after the translation went through, Aleq looked critically at the box of crayons Jeannine was still holding, and then said no.

After another three or four minutes, he turned the drawing around to face Jeannine and the tablet lens the way he had with the wolf fish drawing. This time the colors were mostly black and red and there were a lot of lines going in all directions, and you had to look twice to see that there was someone inside the box in the center.

Branislav waited for Aleq to say something about it, and then finally, when he didn't, told Aleq that the worst thing Aleq could imagine had already happened to him. Aleq waited out the translation, and then seemed unsurprised at the claim.

Jeannine moved closer beside him and put a hand on his bed. He went back to looking at his drawing.

Out of the silence, Branislav told her, "Show him the photos you want to show him." It startled her, but she immediately opened the relevant window on the tablet while he explained to Aleq that some people had gotten sick in Nuuk and it was important to find out if any of them had come from Ilimanaq or had been there recently. As soon as Aleq seemed to understand, she started her slide show of the first thirty-three infected. She had only gotten to number seven when he reached a hand to the screen.

"He says that's Mr. Hansenip, his grandparents' neighbor," the translator told them.

"Halle-fucking-lujah," Jeannine breathed.

"That's it," Hank exulted in her ear. "I'm already texting Atlanta." She'd forgotten how many people were listening in.

"Good work, everybody," Emily told them all. Somewhere Jeannine could hear someone else cheering, as well.

"Tell Aleq thank you from all of us," Branislav finally told Elias.

Elias translated. "He says you're welcome," he said. And then, after another quiet comment from Aleq, he added, "He wants to know if now you're not going to talk to him anymore."

X

* * * * * * *❖* * * * * * * * * * * *

She remembered somebody telling her that she needed to give him her ID and DOB pronto, and the chief attending leaning over her wherever she'd fallen near the admissions desk and harshly telling whoever it was that they already had all that information. She remembered having stayed in bed as long as possible that morning, hoping it would all go away, and that when she'd finally figured she had to break the news to her mother and sister, their shouting and panic had continued for so long it had made her physically crouch in the kitchen on her way out. She remembered registering that in their outrage they shouted their concern even as they shrank away from touching her, and remembered telling them that she'd call, and that they should in the meantime stay indoors and keep away from all visitors, and to call the hospital if they started to have any kind of fever.

She remembered seeing bags and suitcases and even shoes scattered along the roads as she drove in. She'd known her fever had to be really high. Her head had felt banded with a vise. She'd driven so methodically, blank with terror, that the other drivers behind her had laid on their horns and then had accelerated around her.

She was in a room with three or four other patients. It might've been the room in which they'd lost Abraham. The infectious disease guy was in the bed closest to the window and on a respirator. She wasn't on a respirator. She hoped that was a good sign.

She needed to call to see if her mother and sister were okay, but her phone was gone, and when she tried to ask the nurse where it was, the nurse didn't understand her. She thought the nurse was Jen, and tried to say her name, but by then the nurse had left.

It devastated her to think that her mother and sister might be getting sick even after she'd left them, and that the effects of the mistake of going to see them might go on ramifying. Maybe that was what people meant by immortality, some part of her told the other.

She thought maybe it was also a good sign that she could still joke. The woman in the bed next to her looked to be suffering even in her sleep, and Val tried to call someone's attention to it but no one came by.

She realized the wheezing noise was her and that she was continually trying to take large breaths, as though someone had knocked the wind from her. She'd been so healthy her whole life that this was a new realm for her physically, and she remembered with some shame while she was lying there holding her chest how often her patients' claims of terrible pain had been embarrassingly foreign to her.

Other people were wheeled in. A mother who was DOA, though her baby was alive. Her husband was easy to spot as the only person in the hall who looked like the world had ended. She watched him follow the bed when the mother was wheeled out. A resident she didn't know cursed while trying to put an intravenous line into the baby.

Then it was later and she was so dizzy she couldn't bring herself to open her eyes. The head nurse, Janet, was telling her that a Dr. Howlett had called and asked if he should come over, and it took her a minute to register that that was Kirk, and she told the nurse no, and then, after the nurse had left, wished that she'd said yes. She remembered that once he had taken her to his parents' house when they were gone for the weekend, and while he'd slept after they'd had sex, she'd found herself tiptoeing around in exploration, and like in a fairy tale, every door but theirs had been locked.

She had soaked through her sheets and was aware of someone changing them. It was cold when the new sheets were flapped down over her before they were tucked in. The dirty sheets and their smell went away and the chief attending came in. He asked if she wanted some soup, or maybe a little ginger ale. He said they also had sparkling water. He talked to her as though she still had likes and dislikes.

She got him to lean forward so he could hear her. After a few tries, she got him to understand that maybe with her reporting to him what being sick with this thing was like, they could figure it out.

He told her that first she had to rest.

"Maybe we can figure it out," she told him again. She was amazed at how much energy it took.

"How're we going to do *that*?" he asked. "*I* don't have any ideas and *you* don't have any ideas."

She told him that maybe that was their advantage: that they wouldn't have any biases.

"*Biases?*" he asked. "We don't have any *insights*."

She smiled. She closed her eyes, and when she came back, he was still there, though no longer in the chair. She wanted to tell him she loved his sense of humor. She wanted to tell him she loved *him*. He was on his second marriage and had three toddlers but he still snuck back to the hospital once his kids were finally down for the night to help out on other shifts.

When she came to, it was dark outside, and he was looking in on her again. She couldn't see if he was smiling behind his mask. He told her that if she felt a little better and got her appetite back, she could eat some of the pudding cups he'd saved for her.

"Thank you," she told him. She wasn't sure he heard.

She told him that he needed to call her mother and sister. She needed to hear how they were doing. He put a hand to her forehead, like he understood, but she didn't think he did. The latex felt warm on her skin. A nurse appeared beside him and they talked, and then the nurse shook Val's shoulder a little, and told her in a louder voice that she was probably soon going to get more uncomfortable than she was now. The understatement made Val smile again, and as if to acknowledge the nurse's heads-up, she shut her eyes tightly. She was still wheezing, but she concentrated on staying focused on these people she cared about as if working out a promise with herself. The nurse's eyes over her mask looked at her in a different way, like she was now mostly an object of inquiry. The chief attending asked the nurse if anyone had been in here besides them, despite the sign, and the nurse said she thought that someone had, and the chief attending made an exasperated noise and told her that *there* was a metaphor for you: everyone here ignored the writing on the wall.

The chief attending patted Val's hand while she wheezed and told her that the next few hours were probably going to be crucial, and that he thought she was going to come through this and be all right. "Thank you," she said again. "Jeffrey." She hoped he caught her use of his name. She remembered reading someone—Feynman?— noting that it took very little energy to scramble an egg but that all of the resources of science couldn't reverse that process. But after trying to pass that along to Jeffrey and the nurse, she gave up.

Then they were gone, and the lights had been lowered, and she was frightened again. Her headache was worse. She thought about the way they all knew what they were headed for but they still started their days with the hope that it wouldn't be so.

The ward seemed quiet. Somewhere far away she could hear someone arguing. She held still, waiting.

She was aware that she had her mouth open. The infectious disease guy by the window had extended his hand out from under his covers and had spread his fingers on the glass. Looking at them, she almost returned to that state of calm that she knew she'd never retrieve again.

She had to call Lori. Even when they couldn't talk about anything else, they could always find something to complain about when it came to their mother. She had to call her mother. She had to tell her that she knew her mother had been the smart one, all along. She had to tell her that Val had always been a little unnerved by the *devotion* to both her girls that she'd always known was beneath all of her mother's complaints.

She needed their voices in her ear. She needed her phone. She needed to embrace them until they could *feel* how much she adored them. But when she turned her head, everything pendulumed, and the light in the hall swept away from her, and siphoned with it the hallway itself, and the ward beyond.

EVERYONE STILL AROUND FROM ILIMANAQ

After he looked at their pictures and told them about Mr. Hansenip and everyone got excited they left him alone for two days. A nurse he didn't like brought him his meals. He asked for the computer and she brought it to him, but the man with the beard wasn't on it. Aleq tried clicking on the little window where the man had been and nothing happened. Nobody brought him anything to put in his ear. He watched videos of snowboarders and skimobilers crashing when attempting jumps.

The second day he swiped through the photos of the graves. Malik had been put near the main gate of the cemetery and his grand-parents near the back. Somebody had written their names on the crosses, but that was all.

The plastic thing with the sand that went from one capsule to another was still on the little table near the bed. He turned it over, and every so often after the top capsule had emptied he turned it over again.

Nobody had brought him the hat they told him they were going to get him.

The crayons and paper were still on the table too. The nurse he didn't like had taped up his drawing of the wolf fish near the door.

He swiped back to the photo of his grandfather's cross. His grandfather had told his grandmother that he didn't want a cross, that he wanted seashells on his grave. He always teased Aleq that after he was gone Aleq would only notice when he went looking for the gooseberry jelly. His grandfather liked gooseberry jelly on sliced bread and whenever he shared anything with Aleq he always said after the first bite, "It's good, isn't it?"

He always had to have his dogs nearby and said it was so he could hear what they were talking about. His answer to every question was maybe. He never liked how impatient Aleq got when they were baiting hooks for the long lines, since first you had to clear off the hooks that still had the old rotten bait on them. He still used lichen as an insulating layer in the bottom of his boots. He did all his cleaning before Christmas with buckets of melted ice. He used his teeth to pull his knots tight.

He always said he was a hunter even though he hadn't gone out on a boat in years, and he'd turned in his commercial license for a noncommercial certificate, though Aleq still remembered when they had gone out, when Aleq was little, and the way he had broken through ice of whatever thickness with a long narrow pole, and then had had Aleq use the plastic scoop to clear out the loose pieces, and the way when he'd closed in on a seal, doing his belly crawl, even his dogs had stopped panting. On bad days he'd shot some gulls or kittiwakes coming back in, so at least they'd come back with something. When it was getting colder he'd always swung the boat's steering wheel slowly all the way back and forth to use the prow to cut a fanlike pattern through the forming ice. And after he'd stopped hunting, he'd gotten jobs cleaning the school and the community center, and he'd also filled in if the forklift guy had been sick and stuff had needed to be unloaded. At about the same time, he'd stopped going to the dentist, since he'd said it was always just bad news.

The nurse came in and took away Aleq's food tray. She saw he'd been crying and made a sad face back at him in return by sticking out her lower lip. She put a little plastic clip on his finger and then looked at the numbers on it, and then did something with the computer on the rolling stand and then left.

He told himself that he wasn't going to be sad about not being home. By this time of year the sun would be lighting up the ice even this early in the morning. But it wasn't that great. He remembered his grandmother marveling at a young woman who'd moved there from Ililussat, asking herself who would do that who didn't have to take care of a relative. In December, two out of three days the winds kept you in the house. The last boat through before the storms and the sea ice shut down the harbor was the one with the Christmas trees. After that there were no more ships until May. But even before then, because there was no real dock and only the tidal steps on the cement wharf, when it was too windy the boats couldn't moor and sometimes had to just turn around and go back.

Things came into his head, and after a minute or two he used the computer to distract himself. The way the sea ice got soupy before it hardened. The big plastic water carriers you could barely see over on the front racks of everyone's ATVs. The big black water buckets for the dogs that were stuck all around in the tall grasses. The spongy patches of marsh good for catching bait. The dog the dogcatcher shot that writhed around at his feet like a fish in the bottom of a boat. The way everybody's front doors when they opened out cleared away the snow pile outside. The way in winter, hunters could go all the way to Disko Island on their sledges. The morning in art class he helped Malik's little brother paint a Real Madrid logo on the leatherwork of his boots. His grandmother at her happiest sitting in her chair, smoking and not speaking. The time he and Malik tried to come home in a dense fog across thin ice, and the way if they got too far apart they lost each other but if they got too close their combined weight cracked the surface. They'd kept veering toward each other's voices in the grayness and then hearing the ice start to give way and veering off.

He set the computer aside. It was bright in the room. His Thanos figure was still under the covers next to him in the bed. The helmet was missing, but the figure didn't need the helmet.

He lay there like there was no reason to move. The nurse came and went and things appeared and disappeared. There were seashell sounds in the vents.

He'd seen kids run away from their parents in their sickbeds. He'd seen old people go from sick to dead so fast that their relatives stopped asking who was sick. He'd traveled around like he was healthy and he'd given whatever germ he'd been carrying to who knew how many people. He'd ruined families he would have given everything to save.

The next morning the nurse came back with the doctor whose name he had trouble saying, and they gave him an earpiece again, and held up the tablet, and there was the man with the beard, and the man in the earpiece told him that the man with the beard wanted to know how he was doing. And Aleq said some of the things he'd been thinking about. And the man with the beard agreed that it was terrible but told him that there was nothing Aleq could have done to stop what had happened. And that they were going to work to keep Aleq safe. And to see if he could maybe help them keep other people safe. The man told him that soon someone else might be coming to take care of him, and he told them he didn't want anyone else. The man said that he worked with kids to help them feel better about whatever was making them sad, and Aleq reminded him that he'd already *told* Aleq that, and then said that everyone should get out of his room. And then when they all just looked at him like they hadn't understood what he'd said, he said it so loudly the nurse jumped back from the bed.

EVERY COUNTRY WITH ITS OWN SMALL WAR

By day thirty-five, estimations were as high as fourteen million infected. In New Delhi, the chief epidemiologist from the National Institute for Communicable Diseases was himself in one of the isolation wards and said to be doing very poorly. The Egyptian media was reporting a mass breakout from one of Alexandria's largest isolation camps, triggered by the sight of an imam's body being carried out. The army units guarding the camp were said to have let it happen, more terrified than the patients they were guarding. Ukraine and Kazakhstan were reporting hospitals so overwhelmed that even the dispensaries were now shut down. One of the microbiologists at Porton Down accidentally infected himself and the media panic forced it to close its labs and send its staff home for a week.

The WHO's most recent situation bulletin described the challenges involved in mounting a response to the outbreak for those countries most affected as akin to a small war.

And those countries were mounting that response with state health departments featuring no more than skeleton staffs after having weathered however many hiring freezes on replacement posts, and privatization, and shrinking core budgets, even after all of the resolutions made in the wake of COVID-19. The WHO technical officer in charge of emerging viruses had begun the crisis with no full-time assistant, so that when someone called from another part of the world, more often than not they got his answering machine.

There was, of course, still no adequately funded or internationally coordinated system of focus, cooperation, and response. Public policy's position in the U.S. and a surprising number of other countries had been to rebuild the status quo and then to sit back and wait for the next avalanche, as though pandemics were not a recurring natural phenomenon. With no global procedure agreed upon, time was continually lost reinventing the wheel. Additional time was squandered squabbling over which organizations would assume which administrative, technical, and financial responsibilities.

Most hospitals still lacked even the most basic biocontainment equipment. Almost no one was still adequately trained in Level 3 isolation techniques, let alone Level 4. And even many hospitals affiliated with medical schools still lacked the clinical expertise to diagnose rare conditions.

Most countries' militaries had now deployed field hospitals and constructed mega-camps to address the massive isolation requirements, but there wasn't nearly enough expertise to medically staff such camps, and given that radical shortage, extremely inexperienced staff were being pitched into the breach in the hope that they would learn very fast.

Access to distribution centers for food and water and medicine often had to be cleared by force. In the U.S., a sizable minority was still refusing to social distance. A sick senator returning from one of the infected cities caused Congress to issue a shutdown of Reagan, Dulles, and BWI. Seven states had called out their National Guards to set up roadblocks and shut down all trade, and in five other states the Teamsters and the AFL-CIO had pulled their drivers off the roads. The president and the rest of the executive branch had been moved underground and congresspeople were now carrying on their work online. A full brigade of the Georgia National Guard had had to be deployed to protect the CDC from an encircling encampment of violent protestors who refilled the camps as quickly as they were cleared. And three hundred miles away in Jacksonville, a deranged libertarian attacked a hospital with automatic weapons to liberate the patients being held there against their will.

The WHO, which had followed its global alert with a series of travel warnings and then a series of travel bans, and then a series of situation bulletins, on day thirty-six finally ceased its foot-dragging and upped its announced pandemic level to Phase 6, its highest, designating for anyone who might have missed it by this point that a global pandemic was officially under way.

XI

✦ ✦ ✦ ✦ ✦ ✦ ✦ ✦ ✦ ✦ ✦ ✦ ✦ ✦ ✦ ✦ ✦ ✦ ✦ ✦

Sometime in the middle of the night a phone message had come through from a Madeline, Jeannine noticed when she checked her phone on the bedside table after having sat up with the sun in her eyes. Who was Madeline?

Madeline turned out to be her CDC supervisor's wife—of course—leaving a message that he was so sick that he couldn't call. Jeannine had only met her twice. On the message she sounded like she was weeping, though as upset as she was, she still went on to add some other information, about three or four other people who'd been at that party having already died, and some more having gotten sick.

What party? Jeannine thought, then remembered the anniversary party he'd mentioned.

She took a few minutes to process the information, her bare feet on the floor, and then shook herself like a dog and called Madeline back and didn't get through. She made coffee and sat holding her hair with her hands and then called a few other people from her center at the CDC, and they confirmed the bad news and provided more details.

"Every day he'd say after he'd hung up his coat, 'So we're all still healthy, knock on wood?'" one of the lab techs told her tearfully. "He was so careful, and worked so hard to make sure we were careful," she wailed. She went on about how upset he'd been about the protestors.

The tech was the third call, and in the middle of it Jeannine had to stop. She cut the woman off after five minutes and told her that she'd check in later but she had to get to the lab.

THIS IS YOU

On the drive in to work even the teenage boys she passed were wearing masks. The armed guard at the security cottage at the main gate took longer than usual to slide open his window. "You okay?" he asked after she wiped her eyes. He was leaning noticeably away from her.

"This isn't that," she explained. "I've just been crying."

He didn't answer, but he seemed a little less wary.

"Time to make a difference," she said, mostly to herself. Even he seemed to get the grim joke. It was what Danice had said to her each morning in Greenland. He waved her through and she said it again to herself, and then added, "Really." Then she spent the day hashing through numbers that offered up so little of anything that was of any use that, before she ended her work, she drew a slug with a moronic expression on the notepad beside her keyboard, and captioned it "THIS IS YOU."

THERE YOU ARE

One of Jeannine's drearier boyfriends in graduate school had been into rare vinyl and had lingered so long in used record shops that she had often accused him of wanting to touch every record in the store.

In one of the smaller and dumpier places, a fifty-year-old geek with a neck like a stork and a bad haircut who'd been standing beside her in a flasher's overcoat had suddenly drawn in his breath while flipping through a section. "*There* you are," he had crooned, and had eased an album up out of the rack and held it before him as if it were too precious even to transport to the cash register.

Those moments of discovery that she *had* had in her career—like when, as a postdoc, she'd worked out that method of targeting virulence traits without killing off the pathogens in her study—had always brought back to her that geek in his overcoat, standing there like all the time he'd pissed away had been vindicated. All those hours spent two to a bench, measuring solutions with pipettes or preparing gels or working with mice, intermittently apathetic or demoralized, hearing vague stories of how well rival labs were doing and how much funding was headed everywhere else, had drilled into her that some people earned their pessimism while others were just naturally good at it. But she'd never lost the sense that she might be a part of a major investigation that succeeded. "You're a bigger optimist than *I* am," Danice had exclaimed a little way into their time together in Greenland. "You *talk* a good gloom-and-doom game, but you think everything's going to work out, don't you?" Branislav had said a version of the same thing the other night when he'd ushered her out of his hotel room.

AULD LANG SYNE

Speaking of which: she was irritated to discover four emails and a Post-it note at her workstation all from Hank and Emily on the subject of Branislav. He apparently wanted to stay, for Aleq's sake. Hank's response had been that this was a Level 4 facility.

There were two texts from Branislav as well. He was in the building and asking to see her. She told him he might as well come now. It felt like she'd just pressed Send and then there was a knock on the door.

He came in and shut the door behind him. For some reason he had hilarious hat hair, but she didn't mention it.

"I heard you want to argue for staying," she told him.

"It just feels a little cold-blooded to do all this work to win the kid over and then to stick him in a holding room like one of the ferrets," Branislav said.

"We're not just going to stick him in a room," she protested, and when he looked at her in response, she flashed on all of the times before Mirko's death when she'd breezily said to Branislav things like "The kid'll be fine home all alone." After one late night they'd returned to find him asleep next to the door.

"It's not just Hank," she told him. "Homeland Security is on his back. They're on a mission from God to contract rather than expand clearances."

"I already heard all of this," Branislav said.

"What're you hoping I can do?" she asked, suddenly very tired. "Maybe if I went to the mat for you on this I could get you another half a week."

"Isn't there anything else that you or they imagine we might *need* from the boy that I could help with?" he asked.

"I think they're thinking they can always come back to you remotely if they have to," she told him.

"It wasn't my call," she added after he didn't respond. "I'm actually still surprised I was able to get you here in the first place."

"I said I get it," he said. "I just wanted you to see how much I don't like it."

She rubbed her eyes with her fingers and then blinked him back into focus. He didn't say anything else while she looked at him, and she didn't say anything else, either.

"I had the nurse bring him a calendar and a magic marker, and had him circle the last day of this week, and told him that that was our Goodbye Day," he said. "You should have seen the way he looked at it."

Her phone buzzed, and emails were stacking up in her inbox when she glanced at her computer monitor. "How did he look at it?" she asked.

He gave her a disappointed expression again and chose not to answer.

"Where was I during all of this?" she wanted to know.

"I don't know. In bed?" he asked. "Seems like you got a late start today."

"I'm going to do everything for this kid that I can," she finally told him.

He nodded unhappily, like he knew that. He said he'd been interested in administering some of the newer tests to the boy, to see where the boy stood—like the CAT or the WISC-R—but nobody here was interested.

"You know if there was anything I could do for you I would do it," she said.

He looked at her like he could see every failure she'd ever been a party to. He smiled. "You know what *auld lang syne* actually means?" he asked.

She made a *now*-what-are-we-talking-about face. "I don't even know what language it is," she said.

"Scottish," he said. "It means 'For the sake of old times.' It's an interesting question the song's asking, if you think about it: *Should* old acquaintances be forgot, for the sake of old times?"

"That doesn't sound right to me," she told him.

"I believe it," he said.

"I feel like we could've made it work," she said stubbornly. But another part of her said to herself, *Okay, you don't have time for this.*

"And yet here we are all over again," he said.

She let it go. "Think he's gonna be all right?" she ventured.

"I can't tell you how many questions like that, when they come up, we just have to concede the field," he said.

"We?" she asked.

"Therapists," he said. "Social workers."

"Okay, well. I really do need to get back to this," she said.

"Be my guest," he said. He gave her one more look, like he hadn't given up on the notion that she might surprise him, and then he let himself out.

And that was that. She sat at her keyboard and started going through what had piled up just in the time they'd been talking.

She found herself listening for the sound of the staircase door at the end of the hall. She thought maybe it didn't matter whether what he'd felt for her had or hadn't been real, as much as that it had made her *happy*, if even for *such* a short time. Either way, she figured she'd keep making the same mistakes, and learning the same things, over and over again, in isolation.

THERE YOU ARE

At the end of a long day her phone buzzed with Danice's check-in call. She was expecting the usual *How are you*s but instead Danice sounded transformed.

"Listen listen listen listen," she said. "So we've been seeing immune responses indicative of a bacterial infection but nothing's shown up on PCR or anything else, right?"

"Good afternoon to you, too," Jeannine told her.

"Right?" Danice persisted.

"Right," Jeannine agreed.

"So it looks like a bacterial infection with no bacteria," Danice said. "Followed by a whole lot of cell death. But suppose the infection had cleared quickly? And if there was so much cell death, there'd be no residual tissue to study. The cells' DNA would be too fragmented."

"Right," Jeannine said, waiting. She looked at the slug with the moronic expression on her notepad.

"So what hit us was an analogy involving retroviruses."

"Us?" Jeannine said.

"I've been going over everything with Graff and Jimenez and that woman at Detrick—Bonner," Danice said.

"And you haven't kept me in the loop?" Jeannine wanted to know.

"And I had this idea I ran by them," Danice said. "And they've been working it and they're excited about it too."

"You ran it by them and not me?" Jeannine asked.

"Remember when it was discovered that retroviruses could deliver genes that caused cancer, and what freaked everyone out was the news that the genes they were delivering were *human* genes?" Danice told her.

"Yeah," Jeannine said.

Danice shifted to her I'm-going-to-go-slow voice. "The idea was that there was a cellular oncogene that was causing cancer whose normal role was to regulate a particular type of cell, and determine when that cell type would divide. But the thing brought in by the retrovirus was a viral form of that gene that looked pretty much the same except it wasn't. So that the normal form had its on/off switch but maybe in the viral form the on/off switch was mutated so it was always on."

"Yeah, I'm following so far," Jeannine said.

"So what about the possibility of something, maybe even a gene, having been picked up by the pathogen and then being *returned* to the host by the pathogen?" Danice said.

"Oh my God," Jeannine said.

"Right?" Danice said excitedly.

"In the case of a *viral* pathogen it'd be obvious that was happening," Jeannine said. "But no one would expect a *bacterial* pathogen to deliver DNA into human cells."

"Exactly," Danice said. Jeannine could just see her pacing around and waving one hand the way she did when something stirred her up.

"There was that story a few years ago about someone's lab finding bacteria DNA in a sweet potato genome," Jeannine remembered. "And everybody realizing that Aunt Syl's annual Thanksgiving contribution was naturally transgenic."

"And what if that bacterial DNA that got delivered was actually similar in some way to a human gene that controls some process in human cells?" Danice asked.

"Oh my God," Jeannine said again. There was a buzzing on the line while they both worked that through. "I guess then you and I would be on the cover of *Nature*," she added. "Maybe with Graff and Jimenez and what's-her-name. But how come we can't find this bacteria by PCR?"

"Suppose the symptoms were showing up *after* the infection had cleared?" Danice said. "If you're talking about DNA getting inserted, the immune system could have *cleared* the bacterial infection, and it wouldn't matter. In Guillain-Barré syndrome people develop neurological symptoms many *weeks* after infection."

"Yeah, okay, but that's due to antigenic mimicry," Jeannine said. "So in this case the bacterium would be presenting a lot like the victim's own nerve cells. And the victim's immune response would clear the bacterium but then the *antibodies* would still be around and would start attacking the *nerve* cells."

"I think it works. I think it's possible," Danice said when Jeannine didn't say anything further.

"I'm thinking; I'm thinking," Jeannine said. "It is the kind of thing my old microbiology prof used to call 'totally novel.' But why hasn't anybody *else* thought of this?"

"That's what *we* were thinking!" Danice said. "And then we thought: Why hadn't *we*? Maybe partly because no one would imagine it could *happen* that fast? Or that there'd be a high enough infectivity to create something like an epidemic?"

"Fuck," Jeannine said. "That *is* a problem with this idea. How does it *spread*?"

"Yeah, Jimenez is worried about the same thing," Danice said. "That's partly why I called you."

"Let me think about it," Jeannine told her. "Stay near the phone. Or should we do this by email?"

"You don't want to talk to me?" Danice said.

"Hey, you're the one who froze *me* out on this," Jeannine reminded her.

"Nobody froze you out," Danice told her.

"All right, I'll get back to you," Jeannine said. "If Jimenez doesn't solve the problem first."

She spent two hours working the problem from various angles. She even got some input from her old microbiology professor, who liked the idea but also said, "But how does it *spread*?" once she'd gotten that far with what they had.

Spores, spores, spores: she kept drawing little spores on a scratch pad to help her think. She called Danice back without even checking the time.

"So we're talking about something that sporulates," she said as soon as Danice picked up. "If once it got into the body it transferred DNA to the host cells and then sporulated really quickly, you could be spewing out spores while the immune system was getting rid of the bacteria. So you'd have high infectivity before any real symptoms. But usually bacteria sporulate under adverse conditions. Like with anthrax, the sporulating starts once the animal's dead and the bacteria are losing their nutritional source. The spores allow the bacteria to hang out in the dead tissue until something else comes along to suck them up. But why would it sporulate in a living person?"

"Exactly. Fuck," Danice agreed, and Jeannine hung up.

She walked out into the hall and over to a window, and just looking out for twenty minutes gave her another idea. She called back. "Bacteria move from site to site in people," she said. "Like TB is inhaled first and then moves to the bloodstream. But you can be infected with TB but be asymptomatic for years. What about some kind of latency?"

"That's what our group was thinking," Danice said. "But how would it work?"

"If the infection was somehow reactivated, it could move back to the lungs and you could cough out the bacteria," Jeannine said.

She drew a bouncing line from one spore to another on her pad. Her old microbiology professor was emailing with the subject line "AND WHAT ABOUT—???"

"I gotta find something to eat," Danice said.

"I'll call if I come up with something else," Jeannine told her, clicking on her old professor's email.

An hour later she called Danice back. She could hear her friend chewing. "You're still eating?" she asked. "What'd you find?"

"I don't know," Danice said. "Some kind of protein bar."

"So I remember reading somewhere a paper about TB in fish," Jeannine said. "I just looked it up. Did you ever see that paper?"

Danice said she hadn't.

Jeannine told her that the paper had established that TB in fish had become not antibiotic *resistant*, but antibiotic *tolerant*. In other words, the bacteria had survived antibiotics not because they were metabolically inactive but because they had acquired the ability to persist in the presence of antibiotics. That had made the whole question of dormancy—could something be alive but not culturable, because it was in some kind of dormant form?—a big open question.

"Okay, so we don't call it 'dormancy.' But somehow, this thing thinks it's in trouble in the host so it wants to go into some kind of dormant stage in the victim, and it starts giving off spores," Danice said.

"Exactly," Jeannine said.

"I love it when every so often *I* say something and *you* say, 'Exactly,'" Danice said.

"So if the infection cleared quickly enough, there might not be enough evidence that there'd been one. And it's just a matter of whether the DNA would have been transferred into the host cells by then," Jeannine responded.

"But God, it has to sporulate *so* quickly. And get into cells so quickly," Danice told her.

They took another break. Jeannine trooped down to the coffee machine and back. She took her second sip and Danice called back.

"The *nose*," Danice was saying. "The nose!"

"Lower your voice," Jeannine told her. "What about it?"

"There aren't as many *nutrients* in the nose," Danice told her. "What if you inhaled it, and the immune system started clearing it immediately, but it was still sporulating that fast? A lot of what we inhale comes in through the mouth and goes right into the lungs. But what if this came in primarily through the nose and there weren't enough nutrients there? It would sporulate there and then, while meanwhile some of the bacteria could have made it down into the lungs long enough to transfer the DNA."

Jeannine asked why it would come in primarily through the nose, and Danice answered that it might be like the flu, where some viruses stuck to the sugars on the surfaces of the nasal passages but others didn't, because the surface sugars preferred by the viruses were a little different. H5N1, for example, was lethal but not that infectious because it adhered deep in the lungs but not in the upper respiratory tract, so it didn't get coughed or sneezed out.

"That's right," Jeannine said.

Bacteria had all these amazing ways to stick to cells and hang on, Danice reminded her, and this one might have picked up the ability to stick to cells in the nose.

"But don't we have a problem then with why it's so lethal?" Jeannine asked. "Given how quickly in this scenario the bacteria's being cleared? What did Jimenez say about that?"

They were up the rest of the night thinking about it. It wasn't until Jeannine could see a hint of red over the hills from the coming dawn out the front windows that Danice called back. By then Jeannine had relocated to the atrium to try to think more clearly away from her computer screen. The entire building seemed empty, which was pretty rare, and completely quiet.

"So maybe the lethality comes from the DNA itself," Danice suggested. "Especially if it's host DNA to begin with: any sort of gene could have been picked up. Like apoptosis. Supposing it picked up a gene for promoting programmed cell death and that gene then lost its regulatory sequences? How would *that* present?"

"Like a whole lot of cell death," Jeannine told her, after a silence.

"The one thing we've seen everywhere," Danice told her.

The quiet on the line extended until it sounded to each of them like something other than quiet.

"We got a lot of people to call," Jeannine told her. "You should start with your pals."

"Jesus fucking Christ," Danice said.

ARCHIMEDES NAKED

The story Jeannine had always heard about Archimedes was that he'd come to his revelation about the buoyancy of an object in water being equal to the weight of the water displaced while in a public bath, and that he'd run down the streets naked exclaiming, "*Heureka!*," Greek for "I have found it!" Before she'd gotten off the phone with Danice she'd repeated two or three times, "You *did* it!" And each time Danice had responded, "We *all* did it," and even though in Jeannine's mind it technically really *was* Danice's *Eureka!*, Jeannine took her own victory laps anyway, jogging through the dark empty building from the atrium to the top floors and back. That took five minutes, and then she climbed back into her office chair, sweaty and exclaiming triumphant and incoherent things to herself every so often, and started sending text after text to everyone relevant back at the CDC.

BELLY UP TO THE WORKBENCH

Necrosis and apoptosis were not the same things, but the similarity was in the way both created a situation in which everything was coming apart. Once the blood vessels started to disintegrate, the infected started to go into shock, and as the vessels hemorrhaged fluid, there was no longer enough blood pressure to get oxygen to the vital organs. The body was responding as if there was an invader and the invader was everywhere, and so it thought it was fighting its battle on every front, and ended up destroying itself. And in an autopsy, apoptosis might at first present like simple necrosis: like just your basic dead tissue.

And within a few hours, word started pouring in that double

checking was proving them right: something had turned on apoptosis in the people infected. Their DNA was fragmenting. Her new supervisor at the CDC directed her to get more cells from Aleq's lungs, to see if what the cells were undergoing could be blocked with apoptosis inhibitors. Jeannine wrote back that she'd already scheduled the procedure with the boy for later that morning. She asked in a follow-up text how her previous supervisor was doing, and her new supervisor didn't respond.

THE TEST CASE

Another question with the boy was whether he was a carrier or a convalescent, or whether in a case like this there was even much of a distinction. With cholera you could have people who were infected but not infectious, but cholera cycled, and the million-dollar question with cholera was always whether it was cycling—coming back— because of changing dynamics with phages or other elements that were destroying the bacteria in the water, or because it just had run out of suitable hosts and now there were more, or just because it came and went, for reasons no one had ever figured out.

WELCOME TO DANICE WORLD

The next time Danice called back, Jeannine launched into four or five hypotheticals that she found pretty compelling until she realized that Danice hadn't said a word in response.

"You there?" Jeannine finally asked. "Did you hear what I said?"

"I'm sick," Danice said.

Jeannine's chest electrified with terror. "*What?*" she said.

It sounded like Danice might be crying. Jeannine, after she got her voice back, had to say *What?* again.

Danice told her that she'd sent out a thousand emails and had been on the internet with everybody all day. And around dinnertime she'd felt funny and had thought that maybe she just needed a break and had been gathering up her things and had felt how sweaty she was and then had known.

She said she'd just stood there at first, with her thoughts shorting out, and then she'd picked up the phone to call Jeannine but she'd been unable to. She said that at that point Dr. Hammekin had stuck his head in the room and had told her they needed to do a better job of finding and isolating earlier in the process medical staffers who were getting sick, and she'd dropped onto her desk everything she'd gathered together, and had told him, "Well, you can start with me."

He'd hustled her into isolation and she'd gone into the bathroom and looked at herself in the mirror to prove there was nothing to worry about and then had cried out at her own expression. It had apparently sounded so awful it had made a couple of nurses come running.

And now it was the whole nine yards, she added. The fever, the chills, the trouble breathing.

"Oh, *honey*," Jeannine said.

"Oh, God," Danice answered quietly, and the sound made Jeannine hunch where she was standing, like someone had hit her.

"Look, we already know how many people have been hanging on in Ililussat," she finally reminded Danice a little desperately.

"It's like whenever something awful would happen when I was a kid, my mother would go, 'Welcome to Danice World,'" Danice said.

"Oh, honey," Jeannine repeated, aware that she was being less than articulate. "What's your temperature?"

"One hundred and three. And the chest X-ray looks like a snow-storm," Danice told her.

Jeannine could hear the wheezing.

"And just for the record," Danice said, "I think there's also some myalgia and photophobia."

"What're they doing for you?" Jeannine wanted to know.

She could hear Danice messing with something on her end and it took a minute before she spoke. "Oh, you know. Something borrowed, something blue. Every therapeutic they can think of."

"Did you tell them to try apoptosis inhibitors?" Jeannine asked.

"First thing," Danice said. "They're going to try a couple of versions. They had to be shipped from Nuuk."

"You should've gone straight to Atlanta for that," Jeannine told her.

"Jerry's all over that," Danice said. "He's been dealing with them nonstop. He's a little freaked out, as you might expect."

"Is *he* okay?" Jeannine asked.

"Some back pain, some other muscle pain, that's about it," Danice said. "So yes, probably."

"I'll call Atlanta when I get off with you," Jeannine said. "And I'll find out if anyone has had any success with anything else that's been slowing this down. There's a list of apoptosis inhibitors as long as your arm. And I've been hearing about new anti-virulence strategies as well."

Danice sniffed. "Come one, come all," she said. "I'm ready for anything we got."

"*Fuck*," Jeannine said.

"Yeah," Danice agreed. She hadn't had time to let anyone else know, she said. She wanted to use the time she had to work on what they were working on.

"I don't know who I'd call anyway," she added.

"How about your mother?" Jeannine asked. "Your brother?"

"Yeah," Danice agreed.

"Maybe we gotta get some other medical people there, too, besides Jerry," Jeannine said. "Is this Hammekin guy any good at all?"

"He doesn't seem to think much of me, but when things get hairy, I think he's the kind of guy you want to have around," Danice said. "And Jerry knows what he's doing."

"Have you heard *back* from Atlanta?" Jeannine asked.

"Nothing besides all the *Oh no*s, and the news that I'm in everybody's thoughts and prayers," Danice said.

"I'm gonna call Kenneally himself," Jeannine said. "Maybe we can even get you out of there." She was pacing back and forth and hadn't realized it until she paced right out her door.

"Yeah, Jerry had the same idea," Danice told her. "But I don't think they have the wherewithal at this point to saddle up a whole isolator transport just for me."

"You let me worry about that," Jeannine said. She came back into her office and shut her door.

"Be my guest," Danice said.

"You sound exhausted," Jeannine said.

"Yeah, well," Danice said.

"All right," Jeannine announced. "I'll get back to you with news."

"*Don't* get off yet," Danice begged, and she sounded so lost that Jeannine's eyes teared up.

She wiped them. "We need to get *moving* on this," she said, despite herself. Maybe the way they'd get through it was by using procedure like a handrail.

"It's so weird, how it changes everything," Danice confided. She said that she was keeping notes because they might be of some use. She said that the temperature spikes and breathing difficulties seemed to come in waves, each lasting a little under an hour. She said that in between, it was like the way you could still hear the reverberations of a big noise after the silence had set in.

"Oh, honey," Jeannine said again.

"Stop *saying* that," Danice said.

"Sorry," Jeannine said.

Neither of them had anything else to offer for a few minutes. Jeannine went over to her computer and called up a search engine. "Where's Jerry?" she wanted to know. "Has he been able to stay with you?"

"We're a little busy here," Danice reminded her.

"I still can't *believe* it," Jeannine said to herself.

She could hear the breath catching in Danice's throat when she tried to speak. It probably wasn't all *that* shocking, Danice reminded her. When you thought about it, she had a zillion microbial passengers on her little boat, and they'd all been well-enough behaved up to this point.

"You need to worry about *you*," Jeannine told her. "It's like the coaches are always saying: you can't worry about the other team; you have to just concentrate on getting *your* team to where you want it to be. You need to rest as much as you can.

"*Are* you getting any rest?" she asked, after Danice didn't say anything in response.

"Yeah, I guess," Danice told her. She said that after however long she'd lain there sleepless the previous night, she'd ended up conking out on what felt like a big pillow of sadness and collapse.

"So what are they telling you?" Jeannine wanted to know. "Are they overnighting the inhibitors? Does Jerry seem on top of this? Does Hammekin?"

"They're scared too," Danice told her. "The last time Hammekin was here he told me that he wasn't sure they were going to be able to prevent this thing from doing what it set out to do."

"Doing what it set out to do?" Jeannine repeated.

"I think he realized after he said it that it hadn't been the most helpful thing to say," Danice agreed.

ALL ALONE IN THE DARK

Whenever Danice had had trouble sleeping as a child, her mother had turned into even more of a sleep Nazi than usual, insisting that measures like nightlights and open doors were only contributing to the problem. This was before Danice's father had moved out. He hadn't fully supported her mother's regime, but he hadn't argued with it, either. "*Please* don't leave me all alone in the dark," Danice would beg her mother, and then shriek, once her mother had shut the door behind her on her way out, and her brother had told her one morning afterward that he had counted, and she had repeated that same sentence in various forms thirty-two times.

Her problems with breathing kept waking her up. The jolts of adrenaline that accompanied trying not to panic didn't help, either.

As a fourth-year med student she'd attended a class in public health taught by a guy who'd been an EIS officer. She'd loved the way he had started lecturing before he was even fully in the room, and the way he had written on the blackboard with both hands simultaneously. He'd told students when recruiting for his lab that he was looking for people who got there early, stayed late, and hated taking Sundays off. He'd told them he didn't love his work more than he loved his family, but he sure thought about it more. Whenever she'd talked to him, she'd been reminded of what Watson was supposed to have said about Crick: "I have never seen Francis Crick in a modest mood." Once she had landed at the CDC she liked telling everybody afterward that as a mentor he had both taught and caused concern.

She pulled her phone from the bedside table and got on the internet. She scrolled through posts of people in surgical masks, online shopping, or giving Zoom presentations, or kissing.

She had to get some rest or she wasn't going to be good for anything. She told herself that it was very possible that the inhibitors would work. And if they didn't there were other options. When she had started out in medicine, her method when she hadn't known something had been to pick up the phone and badger someone until her problem was solved.

She remembered all of those experimental initiatives that had gone south, leaving everyone to put on their sad faces while they marked down the data in their notebooks. Researchers had a saying for it: If you wanted quick results, you should have become a surgeon.

She closed her eyes and tried counting sheep. Whenever she closed her eyes, though, she started crying. *Think about how Jeannine sounded when you told her,* she instructed herself, and it made her smile. She had a coughing fit, and then it subsided. Both hands were wet where she'd put them over her mouth. All she'd ever wanted to do was find somebody to love and make one or two discoveries that shook the pillars of biological thought. She smiled again. One out of two wasn't bad.

XII

* * * * * * * ✠ * * * * * * * * * * * * *

The night before the news of Danice's infection it had dimly occurred to Jeannine, before she'd dropped off to whatever sleep she could get, that she might be a part of that group that had to deal with some media attention, given their discovery. All media requests coming into the Integrated Research Facility were rechanneled to the NIAID Office of Communications, and still by the afternoon of that next day, her Instagram and email and phone had blown up, the latter so much that she turned off its notifications and had to text Danice and Jerry that she'd just check in with them as often as she could. Danice forwarded her a *Daily Mail* front page that featured photos of the two of them from the CDC website and a picture of Bonner under the headline "THE GIRLS WHO SAVED THE WORLD?" Apparently Graff and Jimenez didn't rate, as far as the *Daily Mail* was concerned. Danice had captioned what she'd sent *Who needs NATURE?* and had added an emoji that Jeannine couldn't decode.

Hank poked a head into her office and told her grimly that it looked like an RV dealership outside. His mask was a little askew. She asked what he meant and he told her that the streets leading up to the building's main gate were already a four- or five-block log-jam of news trucks and vans. He said it like she'd invited them. "I don't even know how they all *got* here so fast," he added. "We're in *Montana*."

He said he'd requested additional help from the state police and that the local police had attempted a cordon that had already been overrun by reporters. He said the state police had told him they'd start cracking skulls if that's what it took to clear some access in and out.

He followed her down the hall to the second-floor windows on the front of the building while she checked out the situation. She could see out toward the hills more trucks and vans arriving, and the flashing lights of the state troopers stuck behind them trying to get through. Camera crews were abandoning their vehicles and hustling along the streets toward the main gate.

The whole afternoon was meetings so the entire building could review the new situation and whale away at her hypothesis. It turned out that a number of her colleagues had also been working in these directions, with Graff and Jimenez and Bonner and others, including two groups in Sweden and one in Germany.

"Was anybody going to let *me* in on it?" she asked Hank.

"Have you *checked* your inbox?" he answered.

Before the first meeting, she ducked outside onto the second-floor deck to have a minute to pull herself together. A couple of people eyed her and a few congratulated her, part of the crew that came out there to smoke. Then she went back inside and retrieved her laptop and coffee and made her way into what Hank volunteered was the agile workspace with the highest capacity in the building. Even with social distancing, there were a lot of people here, and everyone else was going to be watching on screens all over the building. While she unloaded what she had onto the podium, even through all of the hubbub and the settling in, she was conscious of the whole room regarding her while her laptop was being synched to the overhead projector.

Jerry had already been tasked with trying to have Danice ready for Zooming if she was up to it, and while Jeannine was waiting for that call to go through, she realized how much she'd been counting on doing this as a team with Danice, and having someone there who had her back.

"Don't sweat it too much," Hank told her before he took his seat. She hadn't realized her eyes were giving her away. "Look at it this way," he suggested. "Whatever happens at this point, you guys have already made a pretty serious contribution."

She thanked him, less reassured than ever.

Danice's face finally popped up on the screen, looking awful. The crowd in the room made a low, shocked sound, and Jeannine lowered her chin and swallowed as a means of getting ahold of her voice, and said, "Hey, Dr. Torrone! How're you doing?"

"How're *you*, Dr. Dziri?" Danice responded, and the crowd applauded. The applause went on for a few minutes. Danice's smile broke out on both sides of her venturi mask, and Jeannine was so pummeled with gratitude for her friend's happiness, and desolation at her condition, that she stood at the podium peering down until uncomfortable murmurs began to arise, and she only snapped out of it when Danice called, as though she'd pulled together every ounce of energy she had left, "*I'm* ready when *you* all are."

VICTORY LAPS IN A WHEELCHAIR

There was more bad news from Porton Down: they had just gotten up and running again and a lab tech who ran the autoclave had become infected and had infected her family. The whole place was being shut down again and all Level 4 labs were being put on notice to re-review their safety procedures. Hank announced the news at the end of their session after thanking Jeannine and Danice.

It had mostly gone well. A number of problems with their theory had been raised and pursued, but none of those concerns had demolished it completely, and some people had pointed out that what they'd come up with also at least had the virtue of somewhat elegantly explaining a number of baffling aspects of the outbreak. And there also seemed to be a palpable feeling in the room that maybe this was real progress.

Jerry intervened to say that he didn't think Danice had much left in the tank for the follow-up meetings, and Danice didn't argue with him. Jeannine said not to worry, that she could take it from this point, but she did want to hear about the apoptosis inhibitors before they got off. Jerry started to answer, but Danice said, "*I'll* tell her," and then started coughing so much that she couldn't, and Hank found Jeannine a room for the little time that she had left between meetings, and after he shut her inside, she could hear him turning people away at the door.

When Danice finally stopped coughing, she seemed spent, and hung her head. It looked like Jerry had gotten her a bedpan. Jeannine didn't know whether or not to say something, and he poked his head in front of the lens and indicated concern with his eyebrows.

Two minutes ticked off the digital clock on the desk of whoever's office she was occupying before Danice told her that that morning she'd been given the first of the five most likely therapeutics that had progressed to clinical testing, a caspase inhibitor that had been successful in clinical trials with liver diseases associated with accelerated apoptosis. She said that everybody back in Atlanta was hopeful about it.

"They really are," Jerry chimed in.

"How long is it supposed to take before we can see if it's having any effect?" Jeannine asked.

Danice breathed out, and again took as much time as she needed before she answered. "It varies," she said.

"Why am I not surprised?" Jeannine responded. "And are there side effects?"

The question brought a little snort from Danice, who had closed her eyes. "*Oh*, yes," she smiled.

Jeannine waited to hear what they were, but Danice just kept her eyes closed. "So am I going to get to learn what they might be?" Jeannine finally asked.

"Well, let's put it this way," Danice told her, after an uncomfortable silence. "I may be taking my victory laps in a wheelchair."

TURNS OUT THEY DID JUST STICK HIM IN A ROOM

The meetings went on past eight p.m. and she felt like if she had to confront one more skeptical face on Zoom she would slap somebody, but she reminded herself that, to be fair, most people had looked more absorbed than skeptical. It turned out that a group had been meeting *there* about the idea, as well, and when she complained to Hank about not having known about it, he said, "That's what we *do* here. This place is *called* the Integrated Research Facility."

"Well, why wasn't *I* notified?" she asked.

"I'm sure you were," he said. "Have you *checked* your inbox?"

"You already asked me that," she said. He asked if he could get her something to eat, and she said no.

She was back in her office to collect her bag and jacket and thinking she didn't have the energy to pick up either when the nurse technician who'd drawn the cells from Aleq's lungs knocked on her open door and told her that the boy had said he wanted to see her.

"Thanks. I'll check on him in the morning, then," she said.

The technician remained, and gave her a pained expression. "He's pretty distraught," she told Jeannine.

Jeannine rubbed both her temples with her fingertips. "Is what's-his-name even still in the building? The guy who knows Danish? Elias?" she asked.

The technician told her that since Elias was with the support staff who oversaw waste material and sinks and drains and chemical showers, he came in late and stayed late, and had already said he'd be available if Jeannine needed him.

Jeannine closed her eyes and counseled herself to go home. Even with help, it was probably a terrible idea to go through all of the safety checks on a BSL-4 suit as worn-out and impatient as she was. And whatever the kid was upset about, she was unlikely to be able to fix it.

"Dr. Dziri?" the technician offered.

"All right, I'll check on him," Jeannine told her.

She pleaded with herself not to rush, and to be as methodical as ever when getting into her suit. It took forever. Once she finally had her earpiece in and was standing outside Aleq's room, she could hear the crackle of the translator coming online.

"Hey, Elias," she said wearily.

"Hi, Dr. Dziri," Elias answered into her earpiece.

"All right, let's see what's going on with our patient," Jeannine told him. And she unhooked her air and passed through the airlock and inner door and hooked back up inside Aleq's room.

He was sitting up in his bed and unleashed a series of what she imagined were complaints or accusations in her direction as she secured her air hose and approached him.

"*Somebody's* upset," she noted to Elias while she stood by the boy's bed and waited for him to finish.

"He wants to know where the man with the beard went," Elias began, once Aleq stopped talking.

There were crayons and paper on the floor near the bed. A little blue superhero figure lay on its back on the other side of the room. Even the plastic hourglass had been flung all the way under the rolling cart. The tablet was on his bedside table, facedown.

She told him that Branislav had had to leave, and that he'd been very sorry about it, and that she thought they had already had their Goodbye Day, and had talked about all of that.

While Elias translated, Aleq peered at her as if checking her story against Branislav's. After Elias finished, Aleq didn't ask a follow-up question, and Elias evidently didn't feel the need to translate whatever else Aleq had been saying while she'd been hooking in.

Maybe the kid had some mutant form of something that prevented the apoptosis from going haywire, she found herself thinking. Maybe he was just genetically lucky, for whatever reason. Since apoptosis was this whole pathway, during which a lot of things had to happen, he might have had a mutated form of some kind of supercompetent downstream effector or regulator, so the normal cascade that would have been set off was stopped in its path.

"Which would, of course, be of great interest to the rest of us in the human race who hope to survive this thing," she said aloud.

"Want me to translate that?" Elias asked, puzzled.

"Just talking to myself," she said.

Aleq said something else while still looking at her. "He wants to know if you're just going to stare at him," Elias said in her ear.

Maybe it was a mutation he'd been born with, she thought. It could have been a germ-line mutation or an alteration in the egg or sperm that made him. But his family didn't have it; they were dead. The more she thought about it one way or the other, the more she thought it was likely that he had a mutation in his apoptosis regulator.

"I guess you *are* just going to stare at him," Elias remarked, startling her.

"Excuse me?" she asked.

"Sorry. I'm kidding," he said. "I wasn't sure you'd heard me."

She looked through the window across the atrium at him in a way that she hoped suggested a reprimand. "Tell him we're sorry he's had to go through all of this here," she said. "And tell him that he might be the most important boy in all of Greenland."

She watched Aleq's face while she listened to the Danish, and when Elias was finished passing that along, the boy had less response to it than he would have had to the news that lunch would be late.

She felt a wave of impatience, looking at him, and banished it. *Now that you're all the way in here, try to be a human being*, she suggested to herself.

Aleq asked her a question. "He wants to know if the man with the beard was your friend or the person you had sex with," Elias translated.

She snorted, and was going to laugh, but something in her faltered. She stepped closer and sat on the edge of the bed, twisting around to ensure that her hose was clear. She had to tilt her head a little to get rid of some of the glare from the overhead lights on her bonnet. He seemed to be studying her face, and again she had the weird feeling that she wasn't sure what was on it.

She asked if he was still experiencing those pictures in his head of his friend remembering him. She watched while the translation caused him pain, but then he looked up as if he appreciated her having remembered that much.

They sat with each other for a few minutes while she ran a gloved finger over his hand.

He started recounting something, and even Elias, once he began translating, sounded moved. "He says that in his head his friend remembers everything," Elias said. "The good and the bad."

When he didn't go on, Jeannine asked about some of the good.

Elias started translating at times before the boy was fully finished, so she had to deal with both voices at once, but managed to do so without missing too much. Apparently in the summer Aleq's friend had ridden around on his bike with a broom handle under one arm and used it to spear other kids off their bikes. And other kids had started to carry around garbage can lids and their own broom handles and it got to be a really big game in the settlement. And another summer thing they liked was chasing geese and ptarmigan around the heather with an old badminton racket. And it got so that even dogs followed his friend around, to see what he would do next.

After Aleq stopped talking, he seemed to pull back into his sadness again. Jeannine thanked him for sharing with her, and in response he asked if he was right in thinking that he was never going to see the man with the beard again. And if she was eventually going to go away too.

She told him that she wasn't sure what was going to happen, and that that was the truth, but that she wasn't going anywhere right away. He told her that his grandmother, when he was ten, had told his mother not to come to his grandmother's house when his mother had been drinking, and so his mother had stayed away after that, and hadn't even wanted him to visit. And that sometimes all he remembered about her was her telling him to eat more fat to keep out the cold.

She remembered with a pang something that Branislav had said about him when they'd been sitting in Branislav's hotel room. "I just want to give him a chance to participate in a *new* story," he'd said. She didn't remember how she'd responded.

Aleq addressed the window, as if talking to Elias, and Elias reported that Aleq said that he didn't feel well, and Jeannine, once she'd heard, took the boy by the shoulders and asked him, "Do you mean you're sick? Do you feel like you're sick?" But he didn't elaborate.

She looked over at Elias across the atrium. He gave her a shrug.

She crossed to the rolling cart and got what she needed and took the boy's temperature and blood oxygen levels. Both were normal. He stayed still, looking across the room, while she went about her business.

"You seem fine," she told him. She waited while Elias translated.

He put his chin on his chest. It wasn't all that late, but she was so tired. They looked at each other as if waiting for the moment when she was going to leave.

He formulated one more long sentence, and she waited for the translation. Elias said, "He says he's always doing that: wishing for things that won't happen."

She felt the responsibility of having understood him, and instead of asking him to say any more, put her hands out, to offer a hug, but he just looked at her, and turned away.

She was pretty much at the end of her tether when it came to energy. She took a few steps toward the door and then turned to face him. "Tell him I'm sure I'll see him sometime soon," she told Elias. While Elias translated, she gave a little wave, and Aleq called to her and gestured her back. Once she was at his side again, he opened the drawer of the bedside table and took out a folded piece of paper and handed it to her. She unfolded it and it said "*Jeg elsker dig*" in small letters in black crayon.

"What does *Jeg elsker dig* mean?" she asked Elias.

"*Jeg elsker dig?*" he asked.

"*Jeg elsker dig,*" she repeated.

"I love you," he said.

She swayed where she was standing, and flopped onto her rear on the bed without even making sure her hose wasn't in the way. This time she did hug him, and he didn't resist, though he also didn't hug her back. With her hand closed she could barely feel the note through her double layer of gloves. The plastic of her bonnet compressed the hair on the side of his head.

She was helping him, she wanted to believe. She was making him less alone.

"Is he tired? Does he want to rest?" she finally asked Elias. Elias, after asking, relayed that he didn't.

"Well, tell him I *do* need to rest," she said, after she felt like she'd held the boy for a while. And she stood, while Elias passed that along.

She stroked Aleq's hair with her glove where the bonnet had pressed it down. He flinched from her hand and fixed it himself, and when she returned to the door he watched quietly all the rigamarole of her exiting.

When *was* she going to be adequate support for somebody? What was her *damage*, when it came to the kind of simple interactions everybody else pulled off every day? She could feel his solitude spreading out inside her even as she closed the outer door of the airlock. It was like his note was meant for Malik or his grandparents or his parents or even Branislav, and she was the only one left to receive it.

She sat facing the window into his room while she progressed through the stages of stripping off her suit. When she was halfway out of it, she took a break, and shook out her hair and wiped her eyes, and looked again at the folded paper on the bench. When she looked back through the window, he'd turned his head away, so that she was looking at him in profile. And she thought fiercely about herself, *This is the kind of person you are*, because from that angle and distance, he just looked like any other round-faced kid with black hair and dark eyes.

The next day she called Danice with the good news that the 109th Airlift Wing of the New York Air National Guard, which among other things ran resupply missions to the U.S. air base at Kangerlussuaq, had a C-130 that this week was coming back empty and could be diverted to Ililussat to bring Danice home. They were able to find an ISO-POD and everything.

"That's great," Jerry told Jeannine, when Danice failed to respond. He was on the line, too.

"Did she hear me?" Jeannine asked him. "Is she all right?"

"She's been better," he reported.

"So you gotta get all your stuff together in the next few days," Jeannine kidded her. "Jerry can help you find some trunks big enough for your wardrobe."

The line buzzed for a minute or two, and she could hear what sounded like rasping.

"She says it may work better to just email," Jerry told her.

Jeannine felt herself flinch at the news. "Sure; no problem," she said. "I just wanted to hear her voice. Bye, beautiful," she said, with a little extra volume. She hung up and turned to her keyboard and typed, *ETA 0700 for the transport. Maybe I can meet you stateside—!*

After a minute Danice answered, *What's the news? What're you hearing?*

Jeannine caught her up.

How's the fever? How's the breathing? she typed after that.

Fever's better and breathing's worse, Danice answered.

They doing anything for you besides the venturi? Jeannine asked.

Hammekin and Jerry are bonding over keeping me going, Danice wrote. *It's very sweet.*

Your mom turned out to be right. You were the one who ended up being the big hero in all of this, Jeannine told her.

Danice's response took a while. Finally it pinged in.

If this bacterium lived in the soil it could have picked up a gene from plants: maybe an apoptosis regulator that was closely enough related in plants and animals that it wasn't immediately obvious that it wasn't part of the normal human complement of DNA. A gene so closely related to humans that it enabled the thing to cause this set of symptoms.

Jeannine wrote back what she'd been thinking about the kid maybe having some kind of super-competent downstream regulator, and Danice responded with a smiley emoji. And then:

Right right right. What was it HE had that everyone else didn't? That's what all the AIDS researchers have been asking themselves for the last however many years about all those people the researchers call supercontrollers: people who've been infected for ten or twenty or thirty years and have never progressed to full-blown AIDS. What do they have that we don't?

And while Jeannine was thinking about that, the question rolled in again:

What do they have that we don't?

While Jeannine stared at it, another question followed.

Have you seen the list of how many labs are trying to do the molecular epidemiology of who's passing it to who by looking at the mutations to see how it's changing?

Jeannine said that she had, and then told her about some other things Danice might not have known about as well. The list was long enough that even abbreviated it sounded reassuring. If things kept progressing on some of these fronts, this whole problem might start to look workable.

According to their theory, the body was already dealing with the bacteria pretty rapidly anyway; maybe it was just a matter of speeding that process up even more, or, if not, of figuring out how to further strengthen those initial defenses.

Bacterial virulence was a relatively well-established field, with some really good work already having been done for years on the ways in which each pathogen had its own tool kit of virulence factors that kept it alive and killing, and helped it bypass host barriers and protect itself from a body's defense systems. Maybe *all* of that could now be brought to bear in a more useful way.

She typed all of that to Danice, and it took a little while, and after she'd received no response for ten minutes or so, she texted Jerry, who texted back, *Breathing went off the rails a little. More soon.* And when she immediately called, to get more information, he didn't answer.

THE BELL JAR

It took a frantic forty minutes for Jeannine to get through to some-one who spoke English at the hospital in Ililussat, and by the time she did, Jerry was calling her back.

"She wants to talk to you," he told her.

"Jesus Christ," she said. "What're you, the Master of Suspense? You type that to me and then disappear?"

"Sorry," he told her. "Things got a little involved here."

Jeannine sat where she'd been standing, in the hallway, against the wall, and calmed herself down. "What happened?" she asked.

"I'll catch you up on all of that later," he said. "Here she is."

"Back from the dead," Danice joked when she got on the line. She sounded a little better.

"Oh my *God*, are you okay?" Jeannine asked. "You guys can't scare me like that."

"Sure we can," Danice told her. "I was scared myself."

"You all right now?" Jeannine asked.

"For a little while I had a room to myself," Danice answered. "While they were working on me."

"And not now?" Jeannine asked.

"Now it's back to Grand Central Station," Danice said. She had a coughing fit. "Jesus and *Mary*," she said when she finally finished.

"Really hurts?" Jeannine asked.

"The chest is really bad when you cough," Danice told her. She cleared her throat loudly a couple of times, and then Jeannine could hear her taking a drink of something.

"Have you heard from anyone in the Air National Guard?" Jeannine asked.

Danice's answer didn't make any sense, and when Jeannine asked her to repeat herself, Danice apologized, and said that she could barely keep her head up.

"Well, you should sleep, then," Jeannine urged her. "We can talk afterward."

"Yeah, I should sleep," Danice told her. "Leave your phone on?"

"Absolutely," Jeannine said.

And even with everything else she had to deal with, she was aware of her phone all day, and kept checking to make sure the ringer was on. She was mostly emailing and texting, and was informed every so often of even more media craziness outside, and when she finally had to pack it in because of exhaustion, to give her a shot at getting out without being mobbed Hank made a show of bringing a number of people out to the front gate, which pulled the camera crews in that direction while Jeannine snuck out the gate for deliveries in the back. Someone had brought her car around and had it parked a couple of blocks away, and she took it to the new hotel to which she'd been moved. Her things were in paper bags waiting for her on the hotel room's coffee table when she let herself in. She collapsed into bed without brushing her teeth and the phone woke her six hours later.

It was after three in the morning. She didn't do the math to figure out what it was for Danice.

"*Here's* some good news," Danice said hoarsely. "It looks like our Marie Louisa has made a complete recovery."

"That *is* good news," Jeannine said.

"I'm so happy for her," Danice said.

"God, yes," Jeannine agreed.

"Not counting Ilimanaq, it looks like in most places the lethality rate is still holding steady about where we first figured it," Danice said. "Like 39, 40 percent."

"How're *you*?" Jeannine asked.

"Who knows what was going on in Ilimanaq," Danice said.

"How're *you*?" Jeannine repeated.

"I had a dream I was in Carl Woese's lab in the early '70s," Danice went on, as if to herself. "You remember reading about that lab?"

"Vaguely," Jeannine told her, rubbing her eyes.

"I read about it when I was, I think, a sophomore," Danice told her. "I thought it was so cool what they were doing with ribosomal RNA."

"Uh-huh," Jeannine said. She sat up and turned on the bedside table lamp.

"And then on top of that they were working with killer pathogens, and radioactive phosphorus, and whatever else, and just making up their safety procedures as they went," Danice said. "It was like a little girl's dream."

Jeannine laughed a little. "Well, certain little girls," she said.

"When I was first thinking about the CDC, I was thinking of going into Foodborne," Danice told her. "Did you know that?"

"I didn't," Jeannine said.

"It was the biggest branch," Danice reminded her. "And I remember my mother telling me I wasn't going to catch any diseases in Foodborne."

Jeannine put her hand over her eyes. It took Danice a minute to go on.

"EIS must've been hard on you PhDs," she told Jeannine.

"It was," Jeannine said, touched. Headlights from a car in the hotel parking lot spanned the length of her ceiling and then disappeared. "Academic hiring season was before government budgets were set. So you had to decide whether to take a university job before the CDC supervisors knew if they'd have one available for you."

"Sucks," Danice commiserated. "Did you almost go somewhere else?"

"Sure. Almost," Jeannine said.

There was some wheezing on the other end of the line, and then a breath. "Glad you didn't," Danice finally said.

"Me too," Jeannine told her.

"What time is it there?" Danice asked, after a little while.

"It's not that late," Jeannine told her.

"So what is up with the *mortality* rate in Ilimanaq?" Danice asked. "It is *so* scary that we have *no idea* why it was so much higher there."

"I know. There's a whole team that's been working on that here," Jeannine said. "At some point somebody's going to have to go there. Right now the Danes have it on lockdown. I can't say I blame them."

"It still hits me at times: the *shock* of that place," Danice said.

Jeannine felt the same way. "Yeah. Me too," she said, after a minute. They were quiet together, thinking about it.

"I don't know what it is with me, but I never felt like I made a lot of good girlfriends over the years," Danice told her.

"When it comes to what we do, it's hard having any kind of life at all," Jeannine said.

"On my ortho rotation there was only one other woman, and of course we were never on service together," Danice said. "And still, whenever we could, we helped each other. I would do all the reading and tell her what she needed to know and she had all the people skills."

"Weren't you friends with *her*?" Jeannine asked.

"It was like I never saw what was in front of me until it was too late," Danice lamented.

"Well, we learn as we go," Jeannine finally said. It sounded lame.

"It's just that sometimes, doing everything alone just wears you out," Danice said.

"You're not alone now," Jeannine said. "You have a friend who loves you."

"When I first got to Washington sometimes I got so lonely I used to call my apartment 'the Bell Jar,'" Danice said. "But none of my girlfriends got the joke."

"*I* get it," Jeannine told her. "I think it's funny."

"Thanks," Danice said. "I know you gotta get up soon. I just wanted to talk."

"No, stay on," Jeannine told her.

"I'll rest too," Danice assured her. "Then I'll call back."

THINGS THAT WAIT EONS PROBABLY
DON'T ROLL OVER SO EASILY

An hour before dawn Jeannine was awake again and looking out the window in the dark. The first few texts from her mother had been screenshots of the front page of the *Detroit Free Press* with headlines like "DEARBORN GIRL HELPS FIND THE BUG" followed by her mother's exclamation points, or "DAUGHTER OF ALGE-RIAN IMMIGRANTS HELPED SPOT WHAT THE REST OF THE WORLD MISSED," and when she'd gotten a minute, Jeannine had texted back, *Amazing, huh? Nothing certain yet. Crazy here. More soon*, but that hadn't mollified her mother, whose last four texts had been *CALL ME!!!*

She groped around for the phone on her bedside table and slid it over and found her mother's text thread. *Will soon*, she texted back. Her mother immediately called, and Jeannine let it go to voicemail. The little red oval on her phone icon informed her that she now had 1,278 unread messages. She clicked on it and scrolled only a short way through the end of the list before she came to *Madeline*. She clicked on that, fearfully. She could barely make out the woman's voice through her sobbing. She'd been calling to let Jeannine know that Jeannine's supervisor was dead.

The phone buzzed again, and she answered it this time.

"I've been thinking about Q fever," Danice told her. She was clearing her throat, loudly.

"You sound like Debra Winger," Jeannine told her.

"I don't know who that is," Danice said impatiently.

"That actress with the really raspy voice," Jeannine explained. "It doesn't matter."

"I don't know if you remember much about it, but they first no-ticed it what, in the early '30s?" Danice guessed. "And it was reminding me about how *everything* might be up in the air with something this new."

"Okay. All right," Jeannine said.

"What's wrong?" Danice asked. "You sound terrible."

Jeannine told her about her supervisor.

"Oh, jeez," Danice said. "I am so, so sorry."

"Yeah," Jeannine said. She started to cry.

Danice waited for her to get ahold of herself for a few minutes. It was getting a lot lighter outside.

"So this Q fever," Danice finally said.

"It was pretty freaky, I remember," Jeannine said, wiping her nose on her bedsheet. "Right?"

"They thought it was a virus, because it behaved like one, and it wasn't like any other bacteria," Danice said. She panted for a minute, and Jeannine waited, before she went on. "It turned out it was passing from one species or individual to another through super-tiny airborne particles and it was an *intracellular* bacterium and reproduced inside the cells of its host, like a virus, and not out in the bloodstream or gut where the immune system could more easily target it. And it existed as two different forms of bacterial particle, each with different characteristics: one for replicating and one for hunkering down. And it was resistant to desiccation, acids, high and low temperatures, and ultraviolet light. It was *so* weirdly dangerous that *biowar* researchers worked on it in the '50s."

"Yeah, there's a lot we have to hope we're still not totally in the dark about," Jeannine agreed.

"Or what about Legionnaires' disease?" Danice asked. "It turned out that *its* growth characteristics were almost nothing like any other bacteria's. It turned out to be unbelievably slow-growing and unbelievably hardy. How long *was* it where *all* they knew about it was that it had been around for a long time, its most effective mode of transmission was through the air, and its natural home was somewhere else in nature?"

"Well, if the point here is to scare me . . . ," Jeannine said, and didn't finish her sentence. "It wasn't like I was sitting around here overconfident," she added.

"I was just *thinking*," Danice said. "That you know, things like this that wait eons for their opportunity: they probably don't roll over so easily."

"Are you feeling any better?" Jeannine asked her. "Your breathing sounds about the same."

"What we all should have been doing was microbial impact assessments, like environmental impact assessments," Danice told her.

"Maybe from here on in they will," Jeannine said.

"From here on in," Danice scoffed. "*All* of those pathogens that over time we've de-adapted to—we keep sticking our noses everywhere, they're *all* coming back."

"Think of it as job security," Jeannine joked feebly.

Danice had a coughing fit as a response. "*God*," she said when she was finished, probably in reference to the pain in her chest. "Who would *you* put your money on? Humans have been around for what, two hundred thousand years? And bacteria for like three and a half *billion*."

THE END OF THE LINE IS
NEVER A GOOD PLACE TO BE

A few hours later they tried a Zoom call but the image kept freezing so they settled for a regular call.

"Is that your *breathing*?" Jeannine wanted to know. "What is that sound?"

"After you went to Montana, when I would call you, I would think to myself, *What do you need* now? *Why are you always calling her?*" Danice said.

"I'm always happy to hear from you," Jeannine said. "What's wrong with calling a friend? There's nothing wrong with calling a friend."

"Sometimes it's like there's not much more going on with me than needing to talk to you, and I'm okay with that," Danice told her.

"So am I," Jeannine said. "And we certainly have plenty to talk about. But you never answered: is that your breathing? You gotta call somebody."

"I lie here working the problem, or wondering how you're doing," Danice said. "And I forget this thing for a minute. And then it reminds me that *it* hasn't forgotten *me*."

"Shouldn't you be on a ventilator? Why aren't you on a ventilator?" Jeannine asked.

"There aren't quite enough to go around," Danice said. "Plus you have to be sedated to be on one, and I have too much to do. And believe it or not, there are lots of people here in worse shape than me."

"But who's more important than the health care workers there?" Jeannine demanded. "What happens to everybody else if they can't work?"

Danice took some measured breaths as a response.

"Do you want *me* to call somebody?" Jeannine said. "Do *I* have to do it?"

"No, I paged somebody," Danice said. "They gave me a pager."

"So someone should be there already," Jeannine said.

"I'm sweating but I can't get warm," Danice complained.

"I'm calling," Jeannine said. And she put Danice on hold and clicked on the number for the Ililussat hospital, but of course it was busy. She tried Jerry, too, and it went to voicemail.

"My feet are cold," Danice added once they were both back on the line.

"Are they covered?" Jeannine asked.

"My grandmother always told me that cold traveled up your feet and that that was how girls went barren," Danice told her.

"They should *be* there by this point," Jeannine repeated.

Danice didn't respond. They were both quiet, as if waiting for whoever had been paged to arrive and speak next.

"You're going to be *fine*," Jeannine finally insisted. "You just have to *tell* yourself that."

"Maybe you could find some patience at this point for your old pal," Danice suggested. "What do you think?"

Jeannine palmed her face, stung. "I'm sorry; I don't want to sound like I'm blaming the victim, here," she tried to joke. "I'd never forgive myself."

Danice had a coughing fit and then did some more throat clearing. "You forgive yourself all the time," she told Jeannine.

Jeannine had been about to get up, but balked, and recoiled a little against the headboard of her bed. She pulled her knees up to her chest and wrapped her free arm around them. "That hurts," she told her friend, and her voice cracked, but Danice let it go.

Danice asked instead if there was anything new up on any of the data-sharing sites from the CDC, or anywhere else.

"I'm looking at some of them right now," Jeannine said, waking her laptop. She kept it beside her on the double bed.

"So am I," Danice said.

"It's pretty early here," Jeannine reminded her. "Should be something soon."

Danice coughed and coughed and then finally stopped. Jeannine could hear her attempting deep breaths. "You don't have many more friends than *I* do, do you?" Danice finally asked.

"Why are we talking about this? Hold on a sec," Jeannine told her, and tried the hospital and Jerry again.

"You know what I wish?" Danice said, once they were connected again. "I wish I'd been kinder."

"You might be the kindest person I've ever met," Jeannine told her.

Danice made a skeptical sound. "Thank you," she said.

"If I don't get through to somebody soon there I'm going to fucking fly there myself," Jeannine said.

"I always thought it was great that Greenlanders celebrate their birthdays *and* the birthdays of everyone they're named after," Danice said. "And they get gifts from those families as well. We went over to this widower's house to bring him in because he was sick, and his whole house was decorated with taped-up pictures of all the kids in the settlement named after his wife."

"You sound so *sad*," Jeannine said.

"Oh, listen," Danice told her. "The end of the line is never a good place to be."

"Stop talking like that," Jeannine told her.

"What was the *one* main thing they taught us about doing epidemiology globally?" Danice asked. "It was that successful coalitions involving organizations like ours had to share any number of characteristics, the *first* being a clear vision of the last stages of the journey."

Jeannine couldn't respond. Danice said, "Jerry and I refer to you as 'Ms. Saqqaq,' by the way."

"Saqqaq?" Jeannine was able to ask. "What's that?"

"Greenlandic for 'the sunny side.' The sunny side is south-facing land," Danice told her.

"*Get* this motherfucker," she added, with some vehemence. She coughed, even more violently than before. "Don't give up on it now."

"We'll get it *together*," Jeannine responded, but she could barely make herself understood.

Danice rested for a little while, and they were quiet, lingering on the line. She said she'd heard this great thing from one of the male nurses. She said that he'd told her that during open-water season, once a seal dove down, all you could do was switch off the outboard and wait. The idea was to imagine it swimming and to think your way to the spot where it was going to come back up for air.

"Don't leave me," Jeannine told her. "I'm not going to be able to *do* this without you."

"I'm toasting you right now," Danice said hoarsely. "With my little water bottle."

"I'm toasting you, too," Jeannine told her, holding up a hotel glass. Her eyes were so teary she couldn't see. "Here's to you."

"Here's to you," Danice said.

THE TUNNEL AT THE END OF THE LIGHT

A few hours later, Jerry called her to tell her that Danice was dead. Jeannine had fallen back asleep, and didn't even feel fully awake while he was telling her. He said he didn't think he should text, and she kept crying *No*.

She got louder after he hung up, and after a few minutes her neighbor in the next room over pounded on the wall.

The sun was a little higher by the time she got more of a hold on herself. She didn't go in to work. She spent some time standing by the paper bags holding her things on the coffee table.

Why had she gone to sleep? Why had she let her friend off the line? Why hadn't she been there for that instant when Danice had been the most frightened and alone?

She climbed back into bed and sat there like someone who was going to carry on that day, like the worst could happen to her and she could still just roll up her sleeves and work.

It killed her to think of Danice unattended in those last moments all the way out in the middle of nowhere. It killed her to think that she hadn't reacted more to the already-gone sound in Danice's voice.

She realized she was stroking her cheek with her four spread fingers. What was that term for what babies did? she thought. *Self-soothing.*

It killed her to think that she was still paying attention to being alive.

Her phone buzzed. Her computer pinged.

She was going to be there for Aleq. Wherever this went, from here on in, he was going to know she was there for him.

She went into the bathroom and turned on the shower and then turned it off again. She dragged herself in front of her computer and got on her email and put her bleary face beside the screen, and cried out again at seeing Danice in her inbox. The subject line was *OH FUCK.*

Horrible horrible horrible thought: we're assuming immunity for all those who've been infected and survived, but it's possible their immunity won't last forever. The same way we know now that immunity to cholera, for those who survived it, only lasts a couple of months. The same with syphilis, though it has a longer cycle. Suppose the convalescents and other people so far unaffected are asymptomatic carriers, like your friend the kid, and only TEMPORARILY immune?

The email's time stamp was an hour after Jeannine had gotten off the phone. Even as agonized and unable to concentrate as she was, the force of what her friend was telling her pushed her physically back against the headboard again.

"Oh no no no," she said. And some part of her was thinking that it couldn't be this on top of everything else.

And what about the SPORES? Don't know if you saw the reports from hospitals

Reykjavík and Rochester and I think Baltimore saying spores every-
where
   Swabs from bedframes and walls all testing positive even after
   all the bleach and cleaning and everything else. I was like, you KID-
DING me? Thought of that German EColi outbreak where it turned out
the variant was able to stick way better to things than EColi was supposed
to. Everyone was like: how could all these people have gotten sick when
EColi doesn't stick to doorknobs? Except this version did

There was a second and final email, sent a few minutes later.

   Or that other bug that passed through NIH hospitals that turned out to
   stick to respirators and survive all standard procedures for cleaning. We
   should
     lu;p

She scrolled again through the rest of her emails but that was it.

She closed her eyes but she was still there when she opened them a minute later. She had that feeling she sometimes had in war movies when the guy has hit the trip wire but the booby trap hasn't yet gone off. Like what animals probably felt under deadfall traps in the instant before everything was set into motion.

She didn't know who to call first. She touched a finger to Danice's email address on the screen.

She'd told herself the whole time she'd been in Montana that she wasn't really expected to know what was going on with Danice from moment to moment. But she also knew that it had occurred to her as early as the flight out of Greenland that not being expected to know had been one of the main advantages of leaving. And now, whatever she'd imagined to be, in her taking-everything-for-granted way, the indispensability of what they'd made together, her memory of it was the only version remaining.

IT WILL ALWAYS BE THE MICROBES
THAT HAVE THE LAST WORD

The organism that kills too quickly creates a crisis for itself, since it requires a live host, but the effective super-pathogen doesn't need to *spare* its host; it just needs to have not burned its bridges before it has crossed them.

In the case of a pathogen sporulating so efficiently, more and more seemingly healthy people might eventually be revealed to have been, in fact, infected. In a case like that, it would be as if the pathogen had figured out a way of making human beings amplifier hosts for one another. And if an outbreak is measured by multiplying the density of susceptible individuals by the density of the infectious, with the recovered and the immune *not* figuring into the equation, if the recovered and the immune were to *reenter* both of those categories— the susceptible and the infected—everything would then escalate exponentially.

There had been one morning, well before Danice must have become infected, and a few days before Jeannine had accompanied Aleq back to the U.S., when Aleq had begged for some time outside, and they had arranged for his entire bed and isolation module to be wheeled next to a window, and she and Danice had arranged some folding chairs where he could see them and together they had sat watching the ferries come and go for a full hour while he had occasionally put his hand up near the plastic beside the window glass as if to feel the air. The ferries had still been running, though the crews weren't being allowed off at the other ports, and just supplies and medical personnel were allowed on.

She remembered that it had been cool and drizzly but warm enough for short sleeves in the sun at the back of the hospital. A disheveled man in a puffy coat and flip-flops with no pants had stood defiantly on the porch of the house over by the church and had watched them. Some ivory gulls pecking at something beat their wings on the frozen dirt in front of him. Down below in the harbor, a hunter must have had a big night the night before, because all sorts of people were making their way to his boat carrying plastic buckets or bags.

A few fishermen near him were starting their outboards, and even from where she sat she could see Aleq watching them. He seemed pleased by each plume of blue smoke that followed when an engine sputtered and turned over. He smiled and called to Jeannine loudly enough that she could faintly hear his Danish, and she smiled back at him.

"He seems pretty attached to you," Danice told her.

Jeannine answered that at this point she was happy to see him enjoy anything. He made a circle with his hand and held it to his eye like an eyepiece.

The plastic folding chairs that Danice had carried out had had metal legs that screeched on the stone when they shifted their weight.

They had just admitted a pair of women, one of whom was inconsolable because of the way her friend had been infected. Her friend was pregnant but had refused to stay away when the first woman had gotten sick, and had instead continued to bring her warm meals and had made herself a bed on the floor beside the first woman's bed. And now here they both were, spiking fevers.

Jeannine had told the first woman through a nurse that they were both going to get well, but the first woman clearly hadn't believed her. What had finally calmed her down was being assigned the bed next to her friend, and being able to find her friend's hand across the space.

"It is *so* beautiful today," Danice remarked, staring out over the water.

"Blue sky, all the way out," Jeannine agreed. She could see Aleq sitting up with his back to the plastic and his eyes closed to the sun, like a sunbather.

"It *is* kind of amazing that we've been able to *see* all of this," Danice said. "I mean: *Greenland.* I never thought I'd see *Greenland.*"

"Is that a beer?" Jeannine asked her. "At ten in the morning?"

"Hammekin says that beer opens the mind," Danice told her. "I'm inclined to agree."

"Bottoms up," Jeannine told her, and Danice took a swig.

"One of the things I've been really, really grateful for, over the years," Danice said, "is that when I *have* gotten really drunk, I've always been alone."

"Because you get sick, or because you get embarrassing?" Jeannine asked.

"Both," Danice admitted.

They were distracted by some howling dogs up the hill to their left who'd gotten tangled where they'd been tied next to the sled they'd be pulling that winter. Aleq called out something that seemed to be about that, and Jeannine gave him a smile and a shrug.

"Did you see that email from Bustamonte in Atlanta?" she asked Danice.

"I don't know about you, but for me the problem with being an overachiever is always having to watch underachievers come up with shit that's so casually brilliant," Danice said.

"I guess he just made really good use of the time he was left alone with his thoughts," Jeannine told her.

Danice laughed. They'd first really bonded when waiting in Reykjavík's tiny domestic airport for their flight to Ililussat, when it had felt like every four feet they'd been confronted by an Air Iceland luggage stand demonstrating the acceptable size for carry-ons and labeled in English "Did You Leave Room for Memories?" and Danice had found even more inexplicably hilarious a hideous abstract mural overwritten in English in flowery script "That Time I Was Left Alone with My Thoughts." "Yep, that's about what my thoughts *would* look like," she had snorted.

Jeannine found herself wishing she had her own beer, and Danice took another slug of hers. "Can I just say here and now what a *relief* it's been to *be* with someone with a functioning sense of humor?" she asked after she swallowed. In the distance some whale flukes rose and slipped back under, and they pointed at them together.

"Can I just say you're one of the funniest people I've ever met?" Jeannine told her.

Danice seemed to be working something through while she gazed out at everything before her. She tried a number of times to begin another comment, and kept shutting herself down. Jeannine held her palm up facing Aleq, and Aleq, uncomprehending, waved uncertainly.

"Back before Christmas," Danice finally said, "I had a crush on my Pilates instructor, and the day I was going to say something this six-foot Millennial showed up with dark red lipstick and a pageboy haircut and Prada spike heels, and that was the end of that. I think he was in love by the time Prada Girl had changed into her Nikes."

"Well, that wasn't about you," Jeannine told her.

Danice snorted. "My mother used to say that *my* scuzzy little secret was that as far as *I* was concerned, *everything* was about me."

Jeannine laughed. "Thanks, Mom," she said.

"Exactly," Danice said. And she tilted her head toward Jeannine, who did the same. She could smell Danice's shampoo. On the other side of the window Aleq leaned forward as well, so that his forehead was straining against the plastic.

"So what'd you bring us for lunch?" Danice wanted to know.

"Wait till you see," Jeannine told her.

TEAR UP YOUR HOUSES FROM THEIR FOUNDATIONS

The woman had told him that she wasn't going anywhere and then he hadn't seen her for two days, but then she had come back, and she had told him that she wasn't going anywhere after that. Other people did things to him when they came in and didn't ask if he wanted his earpiece in. One nurse told him to put it on, but just to ask how he was feeling. He could see more fear in their faces, but he couldn't locate what had changed.

The woman after she came back again sat with him for the whole morning, holding his hand. They were quiet. She caught him peeking at her and took his face in her gloved palms and got as close to it as she could in her suit. "She says you're not going to be alone anymore," the voice in his ear told him, and he took in what she said and put his hand up to her face shield. She kept talking, and the voice added that the man with the beard was going to call from wherever he was, so he and Aleq could see each other. And if they couldn't figure out how, maybe he'd call on the woman's phone when she was visiting Aleq.

Around lunchtime she stood up and put her hand to the side of her helmet like she wanted to concentrate on what they were telling her, and then she said something to him, and the voice told him that she had to go but she'd be back as soon as she could.

Nobody brought him lunch, or dinner. With so much time to himself, he remembered things he would have thought he wouldn't have remembered. He remembered his hands in fish bones and in cold water and on rough stone. He remembered how Malik's house was bordered on one side by ragged arctic willows one or two feet tall. The way in melting snow they liked to walk in the wet lines made by other people's tires. The time in the flat area behind the church they watched the soccer game between the Temperance Society and the drinkers. The time they'd scraped away some lichen to leave their names and the date under an overhanging rock. He remembered the other rock, and thought that if the woman came back he'd tell her about the smell.

He remembered mornings at the water's edge down by their little beach when the surface was so still that the swell there didn't stir a grain of sand. The settlement's word for that bay meant "where the whales are" because farther out even during the winter it stayed ice-free, giving the whales a place to breathe. One time after Aleq had asked to go out with Malik's family when the ammassat were running, Malik's father had told him no, because the preferred form of cooperation on a boat was between a father and a son. To make it up to Aleq, a week or so later when Malik's father and older brother were off on a hunting trip, Malik had brought the Zodiac around to their beach, and Aleq had jumped in, and they had gone all the way out toward Disko Island to the very edge of an iceberg at least as long as their settlement, which even Aleq knew was crazy dangerous. They had tried to see if they could tie onto it with a line and an ice pick, but the house-sized front part of the iceberg had kept starting to roll, petrifying them and nearly swamping the Zodiac, and they finally had had to just back away, and to let it float off.

And when on the ride back he had told Malik he was sorry he had asked Malik's father to take him out, Malik had told him that if you didn't make some noise, no one would ever do anything for you. And when he'd thanked Malik again, his friend had given him such a look that it had made him think that maybe Malik had been right to have been leery of the gift of himself that Aleq had always been so desperate to give.

He was glad the woman was coming back. He was glad she'd told him that she'd keep coming back. He was glad to think he might hear from the man with the beard again.

When they'd gotten home from their Zodiac trip, Malik's mother had made them go to Sunday services. And the minister had been a new minister who they hadn't seen before. And he had wanted to talk about the big storm that had wrecked some of the houses and washed the concrete steps from the wharf.

He said he wondered why they didn't believe they'd been commanded by the shaking of the supposedly solid rock to heed the angry voice of God. He asked if they thought their God would tear up their houses from their foundations and bury them in the ruins for no reason. He asked if it had occurred to them that they might receive their summons to step into eternity without any warning. He said that some storms were so terrible that it was as if God had decided to punish the sins of many years in a single day. He warned that a storm like that was a challenge to their intelligence that they must accept. And he said that in a place called Lisbon, after one such storm, the king had cried out that he didn't know what he should do next, and that one of his ministers had finally answered that before they could make whatever other changes they needed to make, they first had to bury the dead, and feed the living.

ACKNOWLEDGMENTS

This novel could not have existed, or would have existed in a much more diminished form, without critically important contributions from the following sources: Douglas I. Johnson's *Bacterial Pathogens and Their Virulence Factors;* John Booss and Marilyn J. August's *To Catch a Virus;* Elizabeth W. Etheridge's *Sentinel for Health: A History of the Centers for Disease Control;* Andrew T. Price-Smith's *Contagion and Chaos: Disease, Ecology, and National Security in the Era of Globalization;* William H. Foege's *House on Fire: The Fight to Eradicate Smallpox* and *The Fears of the Rich, the Needs of the Poor: My Years at the CDC;* Maryn McKenna's *Beating Back the Devil: On the Front Lines with the Disease Detectives of the Epidemic Intelligence Service;* Alan Sipress's *The Fatal Strain: On the Trail of Avian Flu and the Coming Pandemic;* Joseph B. McCormick, M.D., and Susan Fisher-Hoch, M.D.'s *Level 4: Virus Hunters of the CDC;* David Quammen's *The Tangled Tree: A Radical New History of Life,* and *Spillover: Animal Infections and the Next Human Pandemic;* Sonia Shah's *Pandemic: Tracking Contagions, from Cholera to Ebola and Beyond;* Mary Guinan, M.D.'s *Adventures of a Female Medical Detective: In Pursuit of Smallpox and AIDS;* Peter Piot's *No Time to Lose: A Life in Pursuit of Deadly Viruses;* Frank Ryan, M.D.'s *Virus X: Tracking the New Killer Plagues;* Alan P. Zelicoff, M.D., and Michael Bellomo's *Microbe: Are We Ready for the Next Plague?; Disaster Epidemiology: Meth-*

ods and Applications, Jennifer A. Horney, ed.; *Emerging Infectious Diseases: Trends and Issues,* Felissa R. Lashley and Jerry D. Durham, eds.; *Emerging Viruses,* Stephen S. Morse, ed.; The First Session of the 109th Congress's *Hearing Before the Subcommittee on Bioterrorism and Public Health Preparedness;* Jens Dahl's *Saqqaq: An Inuit Hunting Community in the Modern World;* Marc Nuttall's *Arctic Homeland: Kinship, Community and Development in Northwest Greenland;* the Minority Rights Group's *Polar Peoples: Self-Determination and Development;* Shelley Wright's *Our Ice Is Vanishing: A History of Inuit, Newcomers, and Climate Change;* Tété-Michel Kpomassie's *An African in Greenland;* William E. Glassley's *A Wilder Time: Notes from a Geologist at the Edge of the Greenland Ice;* John D. Costello and Scott O. Rogers's *Life in Ancient Ice;* and Gretel Ehrlich's *This Cold Heaven: Seven Seasons in Greenland.*

I'm also hugely indebted to Ed Struzik's "Is Warming Bringing a Wave of New Diseases to Arctic Wildlife?" in *Yale Environment 360;* Avrion Mitchison's "Will We Survive?" in *Scientific American;* Lisa Monaco and Vin Gupta's "The Next Pandemic Will Be Arriving Shortly," in *Foreign Policy;* Michael Specter's "The Doomsday Strain" in *The New Yorker;* Robinson Meyer's "The Zombie Diseases of Climate Change" in *The Atlantic;* Maurice Walsh's "You Can't Live in a Museum: The Battle for Greenland's Uranium" in *The Guardian;* Stephen Pax Leonard's "Greenland's Race for Minerals Threatens Culture on the Edge of Existence" in *The Guardian;* James Fletcher's "Mining in Greenland: A Country Divided" on *BBC World Service;* Matt Birney's "Rare Earths Permitting Hurdle Ready to Fall for Greenland" in *The West Australian;* Katie Pieper's "The Unique Genetic Variation of the Greenlandic Inuit Population Could Help Find Novel Disease Associations" in *Genes to Genomes;* Amesh A. Adalja, M.D.'s "Anthrax-like Disease Caused by *Bacillus cereus*" in *Clinician's Biosecurity News;* Jay Walker's "Civil Society's Role in a Public Health Crisis" in *Issues.org;* Annie Rogers's *A Shining Affliction: A Story of Harm and Healing in Psychotherapy;* Alice Barber's *Blue Butterfly Open;* Joyce McDougall's *Dialogue With Sammy: A Psychoanalytic Contribution to the Understanding of Child Psychosis;* Amber Robins, M.D.'s *The Chronicles of Women in White Coats;* and of course, any number of utterly invaluable papers and studies and synopses and lessons on the Centers for Disease Control and Prevention's website: cdc.gov.

I also owe an enormous debt of gratitude to any number of new friends in Greenland who did so much to help this book on its way. In Ilulissat, that includes Dr. Peter Vedsted and Dr. Nikolai Hughes, as well as Eyð Petersen, Stellan Holmelund Fly, Karoline Nikolajsen, and Sanningasoq Tungujortoq, while in Ilimanaq, that includes Kim Schytz, Pernille Neve, and Therese Vihelmsen, and especially Karen Johansen and Isak Johansen, who not only provided gracious hospitality, but also fielded with endless patience my never-ending questions, and shared in particularly valuable ways their community's experiences with the qivitoq.

This is the first fiction on which I've ever worked with the benefit of a research assistant, and that assistant, Gabrielle Giles, smoothed my way and helped me face the hubris of what I was attempting with a huge amount of preparatory work that was hearteningly astute and fastidious.

This book was also inconceivable without the inspiration and support provided by Tom Frieden, who was spectacularly helpful on all matters pertaining to the CDC and international responses to outbreaks; Lois Banta, who was tirelessly patient and gratifyingly brilliant and resourceful on all matters pertaining to microbiology; Fiona Socolow and Sandra Leong, who were crucially informative on the specific challenges facing Emergency Room health personnel; and Sarah Towers, who provided a masterful on-the-fly seminar as to how I might self-educate when it came to social workers' engagement with troubled children. In those areas and more, anything that seems accurate and persuasive is the result of their guidance, and any mistakes the reader encounters are mine.

I'm equally indebted to the saving editorial enthusiasm, intelligence, and resourcefulness provided by Peter Matson, Michael Ray, and Deborah Garrison. I continue to benefit enormously from the editorial training I received for years by example from Gary Fisketjon. And finally, I want to single out for special thanks and praise the contributions of those readers who encountered this work in its earliest stages, and whose optimism and rigor helped keep the project afloat: Gary Zebrun, Ron Hansen, Nalini Jones, and Sandra Leong. And as always, I want most to celebrate my first and final reader, Karen Shepard, who remains justified in continuing to inform everyone within a five-hundred-mile radius that she renovates me for the better day after day.

A NOTE ON THE TYPE

This book was set in Adobe Garamond. Designed for the Adobe Corporation by Robert Slimbach, the fonts are based on types first cut by Claude Garamond (ca. 1480–1561). Garamond was a pupil of Geoffroy Tory and is believed to have followed the Venetian models, although he introduced a number of important differences, and it is to him that we owe the letter we now know as "old style." He gave to his letters a certain elegance and feeling of movement that won their creator an immediate reputation and the patronage of Francis I of France.

Typeset by Scribe
Philadelphia, Pennsylvania

Printed and bound by Berryville Graphics
Berryville, Virginia

Designed by Anna B. Knighton